Sail Away!

Other Avalon Books by Alice Sharpe

Sail Away!

ALICE SHARPE

AVALON BOOKS
THOMAS BOUREGY AND COMPANY, INC.
401 LAFAYETTE STREET
NEW YORK, NEW YORK 10003

PRINTED IN THE UNITED STATES OF AMERICA
ON ACID-FREE PAPER
BY HADDON CRAFTSMEN, SCRANTON, PENNSYLVANIA

For my wonderful husband, Arnold,
who shared his love of boats

Chapter One

The sailboat's long, round bowsprit jutted out over the Monterey dock, pointing an accusing finger toward Anne Moore. *Go home,* it seemed to say. This was advice Anne would have loved to take, because despite the promise painted in gold leaf on either side of the bow, she was experiencing a definite wilting in the determination department. *Serenity* was the word scrolled into the black wood. Serenity was the last thing she felt.

She gave a deep sigh and studied the wooden dock, kicking at a flake of gray paint with the toe of her sneaker. This sudden shattering of confidence was ridiculous; she hadn't traveled a thousand miles to quit now. "Get ahold of yourself," she mumbled, as though the sound of her own voice could shore up foundering resolve.

It didn't quite work. She could still hear Rex Collier, her private investigator of two years, cautioning her that this was the last lead he had. A faraway look had stolen into his eyes when she told him she was out of money, that for better or worse she was going to have to investigate this lead herself. "You call if your fortunes change," he'd said.

That was three weeks ago, and now she was here; the beautiful sailboat with the gleaming black hull and giant round masts was confronting her. Next step—figure out a way to meet Captain Bloom, skipper of the boat. At that thought, the cup of coffee and toast she'd just eaten in the café overlooking the bay rose in her throat, and she swallowed hard and painfully.

Maybe she should have waited till she was able to raise a little more money and let Rex Collier check out this lead like he had the others. Maybe she should have listened to her head, not her heart.

"You need help?"

The sudden intrusion of a human voice startled Anne.

"Whoa, there, little lady. You go jumping around like that down here near the water, and you're likely to end up in the drink. Name's John Quincy Adams, and I'd appreciate no jokes about being named after the sixth president of these United States. Now, as I said before, is there something I can do for you?"

By this time Anne had recovered her wits. "No," she said, then on the heels of that, "Maybe." The man regarding her with a puzzled expression stood about five foot seven, barely an inch over Anne. He stared at her with watery blue eyes set far apart, thanks to an overly generous nose. Maybe sixty, his hair was gray, as were the brows that half concealed his eyes and the whiskers that bristled on his chin.

"Which is it, Missy?" he asked.

Anne ran a nervous hand through her short hair. "This boat. . . ."

"The *Serenity*?" he prompted.

"Yes," she said. "Samuel Bloom is the captain?"

"Sure," he said, amusement stretching his thin lips into a smile. "I like to call him Captain Bligh, if you get my drift."

Alarmed, Anne blurted out, "Because he's cruel?"

He narrowed his eyes as he stared at her a moment. "Nah, I'm only teasing you, Missy,'cause I figure you're here to hire on as cook, aren't you?"

"Well . . ." she said, pausing as her mind raced. What better way to meet Samuel Bloom—to see him, talk to him, study him—than pretend to want a position on his boat? Before she could answer, another man spoke, this time from behind her.

"Quince, you old seadog, how's it going?"

Anne turned to look at the newcomer. He was still a few feet away, but his long legs were covering the dock fast. Dark hair fell across his tanned forehead as he moved. He was dressed in blue jeans and a blue cotton shirt with the sleeves rolled up to his elbows. A khaki duffle bag swung from one hand.

"You're late," Quince said. "Captain's fuming."

The younger man laughed. "Car broke down and I had to fly back," he said, "only all the planes were grounded because of the weather." He'd reached Anne's side by now and was looking down at her. She returned his gaze, intrigued by the gray depths of his eyes. She realized she was staring. Furthermore, she got the distinct impression he knew she was staring, maybe even knew what she was thinking.

"So, Quince, who's your friend?" the man asked.

"This young lady is applying for the job of cook, ain't that right, Missy?"

Anne opened her mouth, intending to say no, and heard herself say, "Yes. Yes, I am."

The younger man smiled, and Anne felt her chest fill with warmth. "Well, good luck to you," he said. "My name's Dave."

"Anne," she said, remembering her name in the nick of time.

Quince cleared his throat. "I haven't told her yet that the captain don't hire women on as crew." He looked at Anne and added, "He tells the rest of us it's 'cause he don't have private accommodations for a girl, but if you want to know what I think, it's 'cause he thinks girl crew is a jinx. He can be a superstitious old coot. Comes from being on the sea thirty years."

"As if you aren't," Dave said dryly.

"Dave? Confound it, boy, is that you?"

Dave looked down the dock finger that ran alongside the *Serenity*. "It's me," he shouted at the figure of a man standing on the stern of the boat, too far away for Anne to see in any detail.

"Well, it's about time," the man hollered.

Dave looked down at Anne. "I'd better go talk to him. Hope you get the job." He smiled before he walked down the finger and climbed aboard the huge sailboat.

"Was that the captain who yelled?" Anne asked.

Quince nodded and lowered his voice. "The old tyrant himself. Come along, girl, you might as well see with your own eyes that he won't give you the time of day." He walked down the dock. Anne squared her shoulders and followed him.

The *Serenity* had to be at least ninety feet long. She rose straight out of the water, her freeboard at midship five feet high. A platform was arranged on the dock with two steps leading up to the deck. The hull was painted a shiny black, with a broad, varnished shear stripe running the length. Two huge masts rose from her deck like mighty trees struck from their forest homes, stripped of branches and greenery, and replanted aboard the boat at a rakish tilt. Now they were festooned with ropes and baggy wrinkles, awaiting sails to bring them back to life.

Anne didn't have time to notice much more than these

surface details as her attention was focused on the impending meeting with Samuel Bloom.

By the time she stepped onto the deck, Dave was disappearing down a hatch near the bow. The captain turned, his gaze sliding past the familiar figure of Quince and settling on Anne.

"Who's that with you?" he asked Quince without taking his eyes off Anne.

Anne returned his open stare. He was as old as Quince, but taller, straighter, sterner. He had a high forehead below the bill of a wool captain's cap, and deep, piercing blue eyes. No facial hair blurred the profound square line of his jaw or his thin lips that were currently set in a scowl of disapproval. He was a good-looking man, she decided. His body appeared strong inside the black cotton pants and natural wool sweater. He looked like he should pose for an ad selling pipe tobacco or ale. He didn't, however, look kind or tolerant or the kind of man to listen to the wild wanderings of a stranger.

"This here little girl is applying for the job of cook," Quince said.

Anne tore her eyes away from Samuel Bloom in time to see Quince wink at her before going down what appeared to be the main hatch, leaving her alone with the captain.

"You?" Samuel Bloom bellowed.

Anne swallowed. "Yes, sir. Me."

His scowl deepened. "What in tarnation do you know about cooking aboard a boat?" he asked.

She faced him and replied, "I've done it."

What did she feel? she asked herself as he stared at her. Well, his eyes were the right color; his bone structure was promising. But she'd thought she'd know once she saw him. She'd thought some instinct would shout "Yes!" or even "No." What she hadn't expected was ambivalence.

"You expect me to believe that?" he demanded, still staring at her as though he mistrusted her answer and a glare would flush the truth from her lips. The fact of the matter was that she had cooked aboard a boat, but the cooking consisted of heating tomato soup on a single kerosene burner on board a twenty-three-foot sailboat.

"Yes, I do," she replied firmly. "I have cooked aboard a sailboat. I won't try to present myself as an expert, but I can cook and I can sail and I do need a job. This one sounds more interesting than most."

"And kind of romantic?" the captain added, his voice suddenly soft and melodic as he painted a picture with words. "Out on the sea, the wind billowing through the sails, the gulls wheeling overhead, the sea whispering in your ear?"

Anne said, "I suppose so."

He narrowed his eyes and glared at her. "Romantic!" he barked. "If I had a nickel for every landlubber who tried to feed his foolish romantic dreams with my time— Look here, young woman, cooking for a crew of five and a passenger load of six is anything but romantic. It's hard work, long hours. There's no time for some silly girl to be chasing some fantasy."

Maybe she was chasing a fantasy, she admitted to herself, but certainly not the one he had in mind. She set her chin in a stubborn pose and said, "I am not a landlubber. I spent every summer on my father's boat. I cooked and cleaned fish and painted. I admit I don't have much ocean experience, but I do know one end of a boat from the other, and I do know about work."

He shook his head. "You're a girl," he said.

"Obviously." She wasn't sure why she was fighting so hard to get aboard this boat. Maybe it was the name, *Serenity*, or maybe it was the captain's hard blue eyes. Maybe it was because she felt in her bones that this was the last chance she'd have to satisfy the craving that had gripped her since her mother's and father's deaths two years before. All she really knew was that she was going to need a little time to crack this tough old nut, and he was getting ready to sail off. That meant the only likely way she had of getting time was to sign on as his cook. If that's the way it had to be, then that's the way it had to be.

"Aren't you forgettin' we need a cook before noon today?"

Both Samuel Bloom and Anne turned to see Quince emerge from the main hatch. He'd pulled a navy sweater on over his flannel shirt.

"I'm not forgetting anything," Captain Bloom said curtly, but then, he seemed to say everything curtly.

"Billy did the shopping before you fired him," Quince continued as he pulled a pipe out of his pants pocket. "All the girl has to do is fix the food. She probably knows more about fancy food than the rest of us put together. This group of high-rollin' whale watchers you got coming aboard are expectin' decent vittles, Sam. Who's going to fix 'em if you don't hire her?"

"She probably gets seasick," Captain Bloom grumbled.

"I do not," Anne said, though, in truth, she did.

"We don't have separate crew quarters for a girl," he added, as though clutching at a final straw.

"I already thought of that," Quince interjected as he filled the pipe from a worn-looking tobacco pouch. "She can have my cabin, and I can bunk with the boys."

"Since when are you so generous?" the captain asked with narrowed eyes.

Quince struck a match and lit his pipe, puffing until the tobacco caught fire. He said, "I figure you don't hire her,

I got to do the cookin', and I'd rather bunk with the boys than cook."

"She'll be more trouble than she's worth," the captain said as though predicting a hurricane.

"Nah, she won't be no trouble, will you, Missy?" Quince asked, but before Anne could sputter an answer of some kind, he added, "Besides, Sam, the girl is pretty. She's what the payin' folks are expectin' to see, not a couple of waterlogged old sea lions like you and me."

Samuel Bloom turned the full force of his personality on Anne. She met his gaze straight on, unflinching, no easy feat. "So," he said at last. "You want to sign on *Serenity* as our cook. Mind you, we'll be gone for two weeks. You'll be responsible for the galley duties, feeding eleven people breakfast, lunch, dinner, and snacks. You'll have to clean up afterward. When we put into port, you'll do the shopping, and when we get to Mexico, that can be daunting. Frankly, I don't think you're up to it."

That did it. Anne lost herself in her desire to prove this man wrong. She forgot her own doubts and said, "Of course I can do it."

"Then you're hired. Pay is two hundred and twenty-five a week. I won't tolerate heavy drinking, slovenliness, or disrespect. And don't bring a lot of silly clothes on board, Miss . . . I don't even know your name."

"Anne. Anne Moore." She watched his eyes. They didn't flinch. Well, why should they? He didn't know about her—

"Miss Moore. This is not a romantic adventure for you. This is a job. If you don't work out, I'll pay you whatever I owe you to that point and put you ashore. It'll be your responsibility to get back to Monterey. Can you accept that?"

"Yes," she said firmly.

"You'll need nonslip shoes. Those you're wearing will work fine." He turned his attention to Quince and added, "And you, you old fool, you'll be responsible for her. You'd better hope she can do the job, or you'll be doing it for her."

Quince pulled the pipe from his mouth, threw back his head, and laughed. With a departing scowl, Samuel Bloom turned on his heels and made his way forward on the port side of the cabin, his steps sure but silent on the broad wooden deck.

"Well, Missy, we did it!" Quince said.

"Thanks to you," Anne pointed out. She studied his craggy face for a second and added, "I don't know why you went out on a limb for me."

He shrugged. "I don't, either. 'Course, there's something kind of determined in those blue peepers of yours—reminds me of old Captain Bloom himself!"

Anne looked at Quince swiftly but found only amused interest lingering on his face. He cleared his throat and added, "Then, too, I don't mind the stubborn old geezer losing once in a while. It's good for him."

Anne smiled weakly. So she'd won, had she? The enormity of what she'd done finally sank in. Victory meant two weeks as a slave aboard the boat. But, of course, it also meant two weeks to find out—

"Never thought he'd go for it," Quince added as he stuck the pipe back between his teeth.

She swung her gaze to the departing figure of Samuel Bloom and wondered—was she looking at her paternal grandfather?

Chapter Two

Anne absorbed more details of *Serenity* as she scanned the decks. Huge brass winches, snowy coils of rope, what appeared to be acres of teak, butter-colored sails, a graceful U-shaped cockpit, a steering station complete with a wheel made of inlaid varnished wood mounted on a pedestal and topped with a compass— There was so much to look at!

"This way, Missy," Quince said.

He pointed at the bow. "Hatch up forward there leads to crew quarters." He pointed aft, and her gaze dutifully followed his lead. "The hatch back there leads to the captain's quarters and the engine room. Come along now, down you go."

This last statement was followed with a gesture toward the main hatch. Anne peered into the dim interior before descending the stairs.

After her eyes adjusted to the darker interior light, she saw this hatch led to the salon, which consisted of a huge circular table and seating area carpeted in dark-green plush. Forward of that was a short hall with cabin doors on either side. Quince gestured that way and said, "We got three passenger cabins. Each one sleeps two and has its own private head."

Anne nodded. What she wanted to know was where they'd stuck the galley.

She did know about boats; she hadn't lied about that. She had always loved them, and so had her father. Actually, Ben Moore had been her stepfather, but he'd spent his lifetime erasing any negative aspects of that title. Thanks to him, she'd spent summer days sailing Puget Sound, which was just down the hill from their house in Seattle. Some of her family vacations had been spent admiring big sailboats. Nothing quite as grand or elaborate as the *Serenity*, but big by her standards. Thanks to that experience, she had some idea of what to expect, but oh, how Ben Moore would have loved the *Serenity*!

The seats were upholstered with deep-buttoned pine-green leather. Affixed to the polished bulkhead behind the table was an exquisite oil painting of *Serenity*, flanked by two brass lights with frosted shades. The table was a giant circle of teak, with a catch to gimbal it so that while underway it moved with the boat instead of dumping food onto the diner's lap. To further secure things, the table was surrounded by an inch-high brass rail. A huge brass kerosene lamp with a leaded-glass shade hung over the center of the table. It didn't take too much imagination to figure out how lovely the cabin would look with the golden glow from the lamps illuminating the center of the room, throwing the rich, polished corners into shadows.

Across from the dining area was a long bench seat covered with the same green leather and backed with shelves lined with books and other mementos of the ship's travels, all secured with rails. Several framed photographs of the *Serenity* under sail were placed against the dark-wood paneling, as were racks with binoculars, charts, a clock, barometer, and six brass-rimmed portholes. A highly varnished cabinet, including a portion reserved for liquor and fronted with a metal grill, sat against one bulkhead while against the other was a wood-burning stove for colder climates. Overhead, morning sun filtered through a skylight.

"It's beautiful," Anne whispered.

"Galley is this way," Quince said, leading Anne aft along the port side, behind the ladder that came down from the deck. She found a small area tucked into the back third of the boat, sandwiched between the main salon and a closed door.

The galley wasn't as glamorous as the main salon and leaned heavily on glossy white paint—easier to scrub, Anne suspected. It had two portholes for fresh air. Hanging string baskets of onions, potatoes, apples, oranges, lemons, cabbage, and bananas swung from hooks in the ceiling and did a lot to make the room colorful and fragrant. Anne knew the engine was close by—she could detect the faint acrid smell of diesel fuel—and she made a mental note to procure seasick medicine before *Serenity* left the dock.

"This here is your freezer; then that's the refrigerator. Dishes up here, pots and pans over there. Dry goods across over here, spices on that rack, paper products behind over here. The liquor cabinet is in the main cabin, but only the skipper has a key, though the guests can get into the supplies they bring aboard any time they want. There are a couple of cases of champagne stored in the engine room, along with one of white wine and one of red. Captain likes wine with every meal, and that's a part of the rich folks' ticket. Let's see, cooking sherry and brandy are right here. That is, if Billy left any."

"Billy drank?" Anne asked, her head spinning after trying to keep straight all the locations Quince had pointed to.

"Like a lonely fish. Must have just stocked up 'cause there's a full bottle of each. Okay, that's your stove. Be sure to prime it with this little bottle of alcohol. We carry lots of fresh water, but you'll still want to use standard measures of conservation. *Serenity* has running water and a generator for electric lights and all. You got everything straight?''

No! Anne thought, but she said, ''Sure.''

He grinned. ''Don't worry about it. You'll catch on, and me and the boys will be here. Billy made a list of the dinners he had planned for a few days. We'll be in San Diego within a week, so you can shop for more fresh food then.'' He was tearing through drawers as he spoke. ''I don't see it, but that list should be here somewhere. Oh, and you'd best remember to put everything back in the same place every time. Boat tips some when she's got a good wind off her bow, and we wouldn't want to lose you under a tidal wave of cans. Well, now, do you want to see your cabin?''

''You mean your cabin.''

''Yours now. I'll get my stuff out real quick. Don't you have some clothes to bring on down?''

She admitted she did. ''I'll go to my car and be back here as soon as I can.''

He looked at the ship's clock—they were back in the main cabin. ''It's ten o'clock. The rest of the crew should be here soon. Actually, all we have this trip are Skip and Dave. The paying customers will be arriving at two. You'd better hurry. Captain likes to welcome them aboard with a light snack and a glass of champagne. He likes dinner to be served before Point Sur, when the sea can kick up and get a little rough. First stop will be San Simeon Bay tomorrow morning.''

Anne shook her head. ''I'm from Seattle, Washington, and my geography of the California coast is a little weak, but I can't imagine it takes a boat the size of the *Serenity* all that time to get what, sixty miles? Especially going south.''

He looked at her and whistled. ''Well, now, you might turn into someone useful around here, after all, Missy. You might indeed. Nope, it don't take us that long. But these folks are coming aboard to look at whales and soak up atmosphere, so we mill around between here and Point Sur till nightfall. Fact of the matter is, we do a lot of milling around. They seem to like it. Besides, lots of gray whales are migrating south right now. After dark we take down the sails and pour on the coal and make landfall by morning. You got it?''

''More or less. I assume you'll fill me in on the details as we go along?''

''Sure, me or one of the other boys. I don't have the slightest idea what food Billy put aboard—you'll have to figure that out yourself. But we do all eat together—that is, the captain and whatever crew can be spared do. Captain's got a fancy name for it. Calls it the 'total feel.' You don't, though. You're chief cook and bottle washer, and I'm afraid that carries over to waitress, though Skip, Dave, or me will help out too.''

Anne's stomach dropped down to her toes. The reality of being responsible for meals for ten other people had just sunk in. ''Okay,'' she said, trying to inject a note of confidence into her voice. ''I've got it now. You can show me my cabin later.''

She climbed the main ladder, and despite her misgivings, a thrill of anticipation ran along her spine. The boat really was beautiful, the sky was vast and blue, sea lions barked from the breakwater. This wasn't a bad way to spend a few weeks, especially after surviving the recent Christmas season, which just seemed to get longer and longer. Someday it would probably extend from December to December,

which she supposed would be good news for her business—
a Christmas boutique—but sounded dreadful nevertheless.
Anyway, it felt good to take deep breaths of salty, crisp
air.

Samuel Bloom stood on the bow talking with two men.
The taller of the two looked toward her, and she saw an
instantaneous flash of white teeth in a handsome tanned
face. Dave. He gestured thumbs up, and she felt another
thrill of anticipation run up her spine, one that had nothing
to do with sailing and everything to do with Dave.

An hour later Anne was back aboard. She'd brought along
jeans, several T-shirts, a coat, two sweaters, one skirt, and
one blouse, along with underwear, sweats, and personal-
care items. She'd also made a quick trip to a small store
near the marina and purchased two pairs of shorts.

A man in his early twenties, about Anne's age, helped
her lug her bag aboard the *Serenity*. "Are you a guest?"
he asked.

She shook her head. The wind had come up in the short
time she'd been gone, and it ruffled her shiny cap of reddish-
blond hair. She ran a hand through it, brushing the bangs
out of her eyes.

"I'm the cook," she informed the man.

He grinned. He had a thin face, a crooked smile, enough
freckles to cover three people, and short, curly red hair. He
was wearing a striped long-sleeved T-shirt, but the broad
blue-and-white stripes didn't add a pound to his lean frame.
"That's great," he said. "My name is Skip. Captain told
us we had a girl for a cook, but he didn't say she was so
pretty." He looked startled by his own enthusiasm.

Anne introduced herself. "I don't suppose you know
where Quince's cabin is, do you? He's been kind enough
to lend it to me for this cruise."

"Sure. Come on." He carried her bag down the main hatch.

"What do you do aboard?" she asked.

"A little of everything," he told her with a shy grin thrown over his right shoulder. "I swab the decks and paint when needed, and I'm in charge of running people to and from shore in the dinghy. Get this—I even change the sheets in the guest cabins and see to the laundry. Boy, if my mom ever found out I did that for a living, she'd laugh herself sick!"

"Sounds like you're a man of many talents."

"Yep."

"Where is everyone else?"

"Captain is ashore; Quince and Dave are in checking the engine. I know you'll want to start putting stuff together, so after you're settled in, I can show you the galley and help—"

"Skip," Anne said as she stepped off the ladder. "Would you do all that if I was a guy?"

He looked down at her and shrugged. "Guess not."

"Then don't do it for me. Quince already showed me the galley, and besides, the captain will keelhaul both of us if I don't pull my own weight, right?"

He looked at her over his shoulder again, a smile spreading across his face. "Right."

"So I'm just one of the guys, okay?"

"Okay," he agreed. "Well, you said Quince showed you the galley. Your cabin is through the door leading aft of it. Ought to be real handy for you. Over here on the starboard side of the ladder is the navigation center, then the captain's cabin. Me and Dave are up forward behind the chain locker. I guess Quince will be up there too. There's a head right through here, but ration your fresh water, especially when you take a shower. The *Serenity* carries over eight hundred gallons of water, but nothing makes the captain madder than someone wasting it. Especially one of us.''

Anne looked at the door to the head and did a little quick computing. ''The captain's cabin is on the other side, right?''

''Sure.''

''Does he . . . will I be expected to share. . . .''

Skip interrupted her mumbling. ''The head! Gosh, no!''

''Fine,'' she said, glad that the thought of sharing a bathroom with the captain was as daunting a thought to Skip as it was to her.

''No, no. Captain has his own head. I swear, there are about ten of the things aboard this boat. Yours is tiny, but there's a shower and everything.''

Anne nodded. ''Great.''

He looked at her, and his good-natured smile returned. ''Good to have you aboard,'' he said. He handed her the suitcase and closed the narrow door behind him.

Quince had cleaned out the drawers in the tiny built-in dresser, but he hadn't taken down his calendar or his photos, and Anne looked at them now. The smiling faces of strangers stared back at her. There was a plaque above the door that read, *Sailing: hours and hours of boredom punctuated by minutes of pure terror.*

Besides the dresser, the cabin contained a small berth, built against the port side of the hull, covered with a navy-blue sleeping bag with a detachable flannel liner. Two horizontal straps reached from the hull across the bunk. Anne guessed she was to use them to keep from rolling out of bed at night. A small desk, tidy and organized, was set against the stern. Anne opened one narrow drawer, saw it was full of Quince's personal belongings, and closed it. There was a porthole above the bed, which she opened. A rush of cool, moist air met her face.

The cabin was in the very end of the ship, and Anne knew the motion would be gentler here than in the bow, but she still wished there weren't a gender problem and she could bunk up with "the boys" instead of next door to Captain Bligh, even if she might be related to him.

Anne plopped her canvas suitcase on the bunk, opened it up, and found the paper bag from the drugstore. *Take two tablets,* the directions on the seasick medicine advised. She popped out two tablets and ducked into the tiny head, looking for a glass. She glanced into the mirror above the sink and found a twenty-two-year-old woman with restless blue eyes staring back at her. "Buck up, little camper," she told her reflection. No glass, so she tucked the pills into her pocket. She decided to unpack later and strapped her suitcase to the bed, took off her jacket, stowed it in one of the drawers, and left the cabin. It was almost eleven, and she had the galley to figure out.

The freezer was loaded with food, all frozen, of course. Anne tore open the drawers looking for a menu. While she did this, she heard the voices and footsteps of the crew as they moved about the boat, readying her for the expected guests. Skip came into the galley lugging a bucket full of ice. He found a small door opposite the stove, opened it, and went inside. Anne heard the hum of the engines grow louder. Skip reappeared with four bottles of champagne and inserted them in with the ice.

"Should have done this this morning," he said. "Don't worry about it—you didn't know."

Anne opened her mouth to point out that that was the understatement of the century, but changed her mind and said instead, "Aren't you guys going to want lunch? Is that something I should be doing?"

He took eight crystal champagne glasses out of a high cabinet, where they were each tucked into their own felt-lined cubicle, and ferried them to the table in the salon. "Sure," he said. "That would be great. Nothing fancy, though." He grinned at her, then left, no doubt on some other duty.

Anne started opening doors. She found the boat was full of food, some of which was quite expensive. Where was that menu Quince said Billy had made? Would it ruin some long-planned future meal if she heated a couple of cans of clam chowder for the crew's lunch? She'd have to chance it.

The stove proved to be another challenge. She recalled Quince telling her to prime the kerosene burner with alcohol. She found the small plastic bottle of clear alcohol and squirted a bit on the dish in the center of one of the burners. Matches were stored in a canister next to the stove, she discovered after several wasted minutes spent searching. She lit the alcohol and watched it burn a bright-blue flame. When the flame was almost extinguished, she quickly turned on the kerosene. It ignited when it hit the hot burner, and she was rewarded with a bright circle of flame.

"Thanks, Dad," she said softly. Ben Moore had also loved to camp, and this little trick was one he'd taught her years before. While the chowder heated, she opened a cupboard door to look for pepper. Taped to the back of the door was a neatly handwritten menu for the next week. She almost cried with relief when she saw it.

"Do you know where Skip went?"

Anne had been so engrossed in the menu, she hadn't heard anyone approach. She turned to face the speaker and hit her head against the swinging basket of bananas.

Dave laughed. The rich sound filled the small galley and sent something primitive fluttering in Anne's heart. She noticed how generous his mouth was, that his nose was a little crooked, his face full of interesting angles. He was older than she by about four years. He looked down at her, his gaze steady and secure and oddly compelling. His lips twitched, as if suppressing more laughter, as the basket of bananas swung wildly between them. "Are you okay?" he asked.

"Yes," she muttered as she grabbed the swinging fruit and steadied it. She was startled to find her second encounter with him more powerful than her first; at this rate, she'd be swooning by nightfall.

"Congratulations on winning the captain's heart," he said.

"What?"

"Well, you got the job, didn't you? You must have won his heart."

"Hardly. I think he gave me the job so he could have himself a good laugh when I fail."

"And are you going to fail?"

"No, I'm not going to fail."

"Good, because I can tell it's going to be nice having you aboard." He smiled, reducing Anne's insides to the proverbial jelly, and she gripped the wooden counter.

He grabbed a few paper towels to wipe engine oil off his hands. "I think that soup is hot, don't you?" he said.

Anne looked at the soup. "Great, I've burned my first meal."

"No, it's okay." He used the paper towels as a pot holder and moved the pan to another burner. He stared at her as he finished wiping the grease from his hands.

"I don't know where the bowls are yet," she said, opening the most likely cabinet door and finding boxes of food.

"We all have our own mugs for coffee. See, they hang right up here on this bulkhead. Why don't you dump the soup into the cups?"

"Good idea." She helped Dave line up the mugs on the small counter. Each had been initialed.

Dave took the last one from the hook and searched through a drawer until he found an indelible pen which he used to cross out the initials B. H. "Anne what?" he asked.

She blinked, confused.

"Your last name," he prompted.

"Oh. Moore."

He handed her the cup, personalized with her own initials. She guessed B. H. had been Billy. How long would it be before someone crossed her initials off?

"Now you're one of us," Dave said. "An official crew member of the *Serenity*. Pretty name, don't you think?"

Anne found a pot holder and poured steaming chowder into each cup but her own. "What do you mean?"

"*Serenity*. Big old sailboat like this deserves a noble name. I've always liked *Serenity*."

"It's lovely," she said softly and then, deciding that now was as good a time as any to start investigating, added, "Do you happen to know who named her?"

He tilted his head and regarded her. "No," he said at last. "It's kind of hard to imagine the captain letting anyone else name something as important to him as this boat, though, so I suppose he did."

Anne bit her lip. "Maybe he let one of his children name her," she suggested.

"Maybe." He smiled at her, a smile that crinkled the skin at the corners of his eyes as it curved his lips. For a second Anne felt absorbed by the gray velvet of his eyes. When he spoke, his voice caressed her skin.

"I feel—" he began, and then he shook his head and left the sentence dangling. After a long pause, he said, "Aren't you having any chowder?"

"I don't like fish," she admitted.

He laughed again. "A boat is a heck of a place for a cook who doesn't like fish."

She nodded and returned his laughter. She was aware of the unspoken conversation taking place between their eyes but felt a little fuzzy on the exact meaning of it all.

"Well," he added at last, "I'll go find Skip and tell Quince and the captain that lunch is ready."

"Yes." She cleared her throat and added, "Thank you."

"No problem." He smiled and disappeared toward the main salon.

Anne took a couple of deep breaths. Really! As if she didn't have enough problems looming on her immediate horizon, she had to go and develop an instantaneous crush on one of the crew. But, good grief, the way his eyes delved into a person and the way his shoulders filled that faded denim shirt. . . . *Enough!* she scolded herself.

Her first attempt at a meal passed uneventfully. She found crackers in one plastic container, fresh gingersnap cookies in another. She dug fresh fruit from the hanging basket and set a bowl of each on the varnished table. The men sat around, discussing the upcoming trip as they ate, the crystal champagne flutes an incongruous centerpiece. Captain Bloom excused himself early and entered a short passage on the starboard side of the ladder. The passage was the one Quince had told her led to the navigation table and instruments, then on to his cabin through a connecting door.

"Sam's got some navigation to tend to," Quince said as he drained his cup. He looked at the ship's clock and added, "Well, boys, the rich folks will be here in about an hour. Better get the sails ready to haul up once the captain gives the orders."

"We like to razzle-dazzle the impressionable masses," Dave explained as he scooted out from around the huge table, an apple in his hand. "It helps if we plot a course of action. It's so embarrassing when one of us falls in the drink due to someone else's fancy footwork.''

Quince gave a short bark of laughter as he took his pipe from his shirt pocket and darted up the ladder. Skip took a handful of cookies and three bananas, nodded, and followed the others outside. Anne looked at the decimated bowls and wondered how in the world she was going to keep the crew full, let alone the passengers.

She set croissants out on the counter to thaw because the menu called for salmon-salad filling. She'd found several jars of home-canned salmon in a locker beneath the sink. Only trouble was, she had no idea how to make them into a sandwich filling.

"Didn't Billy leave a cookbook?'' she asked Quince as he passed behind her on his way between the engine room and the salon. "I've torn this place apart looking for one.''

Quince took the unlit pipe from his mouth. "I doubt it. Captain fired him yesterday. The boy was falling-down drunk, and it wasn't the first time neither. Don't recall ever seeing him use a book to cook from.''

Anne bit her lip and said, "Quince, I don't know how to make salmon salad.''

He furrowed his brow, sending those bushy eyebrows cascading over his eyes. "Well, now, Missy, I wouldn't know that, either. Look on that shelf there and see if there isn't a cookbook.''

"I already did.'' She wished she'd bought a cookbook when she was ashore buying the shorts. Well, it was too late now.

"Can't be that much different from tuna or chicken, can it?'' Quince added.

"I wouldn't think so,'' she agreed. She picked up one of the jars. The salmon inside was glistening pink.

"Billy did those when we were up in Alaska last summer," Quince said. "Good stuff. Well, carry on, Missy."

Guests began arriving. Anne could hear their voices—excited, loud—and the answering murmurs of the crew. She put the salmon aside and concentrated on the hors d'oeuvres, which, according to the menu, were to be served with champagne before they set sail.

Somewhere in the refrigerator there was supposed to be something called Herb Cheese in a Crock, and a container of chicken liver pâté. She found both and then a box of crackers and arranged them on two silver trays she found in a long cabinet beside the stove. Skip retrieved the chilled champagne and took it into the salon to pour. A moment later Dave ducked into the galley and took the two trays with him. Anne was too overwhelmed with galley duties to do more than notice the twinkle lurking in his eyes as he looked at her.

The salmon smelled like fish, which didn't come as a great surprise but did make Anne wonder if she was ever going to find anything aboard to eat. She dumped two jars into a bowl, then added chopped onions and parsley. She dug mayonnaise out of the refrigerator and spices off the shelf. She heard a clatter in the main salon and looked in just in time to see Skip dragging two big leather suitcases down the short hall and depositing them into Stateroom 3.

According to Billy's menu, they were to have gazpacho—whatever that was—salmon-filled croissants, a fresh vegetable tray, and, for dessert, poached pears with raspberry sauce. Anne smiled to herself; there were obviously going to have to be a few modifications in this menu. She put the covered bowl of salmon into the fridge. Several gold pears peeked through the mesh of the hanging basket. How in the world did one go about poaching a pear? She'd serve those fresh instead of the vegetables, and somewhere—yes, there it was—she'd seen a chocolate-cake mix.

Meanwhile, according to a progress report courtesy of Skip, Dave was out on the deck passing around the tray of cheese and pâté.

She felt the boat move and remembered to run herself a glass of water and swallow the pills. She heard Captain Bloom shout orders and looked out the porthole in time to see a sea lion stare back at her from his perch atop a floating buoy.

Anne felt the boat rise to the first ocean swell. The platter of defrosting croissants slid across the drainboard, and she caught it with one hand while she put her foot on the bucket of ice that had been used to chill the champagne and was now sliding across the galley floor. The hanging nets of fruits and vegetables began swaying like members of a drunk chorus line. At the last minute she caught the cake mix with her free hand. Her stomach lurched, and her head spun. They were on their way.

Chapter Three

"**D**elicious!" an elderly man announced. A jet-black toupée crouched on his head like a small woodland creature, but the hair around his ears and above his collar was grayish-white, as were his eyebrows. His fleshy cheeks were bright pink, clashing with the peachy pink of his shirt. A name tag attached to the shirt said his name was Boris.

"Thank you," Anne said.

An elderly woman with neon-red hair and electric-green sunglass frames sat next to Boris. Her shirt matched his, and her name tag read Patty. "I usually like this stuff," she said.

"Is something wrong with it?" Anne asked.

Patty put a jewel-encrusted hand over her mouth.

"She's just seasick," Boris said matter-of-factly. "Same thing happened in the Greek Islands."

Anne took Patty's arm. "Go outside and breathe some fresh air," she suggested softly. "Keep your eyes on the horizon."

"I'll take her," Boris said as he popped another pâté-smothered cracker into his mouth and washed it down with a last gulp of champagne. He took Anne's place by his wife's side. "Come on, old girl, up you go."

Anne smiled at their retreating figures. They weren't exactly what she'd expected. She took the empty glasses back to the galley and started washing up. A minute or two later Quince came into the galley with an empty tray and two more champagne glasses. "It's almost gone. Just a little left." He chuckled and added, "Some of them look as though they might be hanging over a rail pretty soon, though."

Anne, busy taking deep breaths of fresh air by poking her nose out the porthole, said, "If they get sick, don't blame me, because I didn't make it. Did the captain say anything?"

"Heard him tell one lady that you were going to work out real fine," he said.

The compliment would have meant more if she'd actually done anything but arrange Billy's creations. "Thanks, Quince."

"You're not feeling sick, are you, Missy?" he asked, apparently noticing the way Anne was trying to keep her gaze directed at the horizon through the porthole while talking to him and replacing each glass in its proper niche.

She turned to face him. "No, no, of course not."

He nodded. Anne decided to change the subject. "Quince, I feel kind of lost here. I mean, it says on the menu that Billy planned barbecued steaks for tomorrow night's dinner. How am I supposed to do that?"

"One of us will do the cooking outside," he said as he took the last two glasses from her and put them away himself. "We have a stainless model that fits into a holder on the stern. You just find the steaks."

"They're in the fridge here. But I feel as though I might get a better handle on this whole thing if I had some idea what to expect."

"Want to listen to the captain's welcome-aboard speech?" he asked.

"That would be great, but I have this platter to wash and a chocolate cake to bake, so I guess—"

"You go on deck and listen to Sam. I'll do the dishes for you this time. You're on your own with the cake, though. No, Missy, don't go thankin' me, just scoot."

"You're too good to me," Anne said as she headed for the salon. She heard Quince laugh as she climbed the ladder.

The boat was still headed out to sea. Samuel Bloom stood on the aft deck, his captain's hat pulled low on his head. He looked very nautical and in command, even though Dave held the big wheel in his hands and guided the boat southwest. With an effort Anne tore her attention away from Dave and looked around at the other people.

Boris and Patty were perched on the cabin top, their pink shirts now topped with bilious-green windbreakers. Anne suppressed a smile of amusement when she saw one of Boris's hands clenched to his head, holding down his hair.

Four other people had arranged themselves against the cabin or seated themselves in the generous cockpit. They were all much younger than Boris and Patty, and their jewelry and clothes said a lot about their bank balances. Anne smiled at the woman who looked her way without a change of expression. She leaned back against the hatch, prepared to listen to Samuel Bloom.

". . . so the *Serenity* never gets too close. I know most of you brought binoculars, but there are plenty on board for anyone who needs a pair."

"How big are gray whales?" one woman asked. She was somewhere in her mid-twenties, with short brown hair that, while expertly cut, was unflattering to her round face. Her wide-set brown eyes were full of curiosity, however, and her mobile mouth looked ready to smile at any given opportunity. Her name tag read Liz.

Dave said, "Gray whales can grow to as much as forty-five feet. And, incidentally, it's not so much that their skin is gray as they're covered with barnacles and something called 'whale lice.' "

Anne saw the woman sitting next to Liz sit up straighter. She was wearing a blue cap over her blond hair, held in place with a left hand glittering with sapphires. Her facial features were delicate and expertly enhanced with makeup. "Whales have lice?" she asked.

He smiled. "No, not really. They're actually yellowish-white or yellowish-orange cyamid crustaceans."

Anne noticed the blonde nodded as though she knew what cyamid crustaceans were.

"Are gray whales an endangered species?" Patty asked.

"No. At one time whalers almost wiped them out, but they've been protected since 1946. Whaling ships used to wait outside the sheltered lagoons off southern California and Mexico. When the grays swam out of the lagoons, the hunters would harpoon a baby whale, then kill the mother as she tried to protect her calf. Yes," he added as a general murmur of disgust passed through the passengers, "it was heartless and cruel. Thankfully, the species has recovered, and now there are thousands of gray whales. Running up and down the California coast like they do, they've turned into their own best P.R. outfit.

"We'll be going as far south as San Ignacio Lagoon, about halfway down Baja. We'll take you out into the lagoon in an inflatable raft, and it's likely some of the more friendly individuals will come very close. Some scientists say they are attracted to the sound of an outboard engine."

"You know so much," the blonde said.

Anne couldn't see her face, but she would have laid money she was batting her eyelashes.

"I'm as fascinated with the giant creatures as you are," Dave said.

Samuel Bloom resumed command. "Yes, well, I'll wager we'll see a few grays today between Monterey and Point Sur, about fifteen miles south of here. Gray whales have nature's longest migratory path—over ten thousand miles, all the way from the Bering Sea down to Mexico. They travel in small groups called pods.

"Tonight we'll have a light dinner and make our way to San Simeon. You'll wake up tomorrow morning in one of the prettiest little coves on the West Coast, and if you'll look up into the hills, you'll see the fairy-tale castle William Randolph Hearst built."

"If it's not foggy," Dave pointed out.

"We're going on a private tour of the castle, right?" This question came from Boris.

"Yes, that's right. Now, I want you folks to feel free to ask me or my crew any questions you might have. We have simple medicinal supplies aboard, you know, bandages and antiseptic and such, and as I told each of you when you signed aboard, we have a radio and can get in touch with the Coast Guard within minutes. There are three lifeboats aboard, though any one of them would be large enough for all of us. They're housed in those white canisters you see on the fore and aft decks. We'll have a safety drill as soon as we're finished here. If there is anything at all that I or one of my crew can do to make this cruise more enjoyable for you, don't hesitate to ask.

"Now, I believe one lady mentioned having sailing experience and has asked if she can help raise and lower sails and things like that. Of course! We'll be happy for the help, but I'm afraid I'll have to decline the offers of help I've had for standing watch at night. I'm sure you can understand why one of the crew will have to assume that responsibility. That's not to say you can't occasionally take a daytime watch and steer the boat if you know how.''

Anne saw Liz lean forward. Captain Bloom continued. ''I introduced Dave already and explained that we'd be on a first-name basis. The young man up forward there is Skip. Quince is the old man aboard—I don't see him right now—but you can always tell Quince by the blue smoke circling his head from that pipe. Don't worry, there's no smoking allowed below decks, so he won't ruin your meals, which brings us to our newest crew member and, perhaps to you, our most important—Anne, ship's cook.''

Anne smiled at the six faces that turned to inspect her. All seemed open and friendly, even the pretty blonde, whose tag announced she was Irene.

With that, the group broke up. Liz trailed Skip forward to help raise the sails, her face glowing with excitement. Anne looked back in time to see Captain Bloom staring at her, and she tried a smile out on him.

He nodded curtly and turned his attentions to Boris and Patty. She studied his profile when he turned away, looking for some sign, some familiarity in his features, but she couldn't find a thing.

''I thought the pâté was just delicious,'' a woman said.

Anne turned to face one of the women guests. She was tiny, with long, black hair elaborately braided and wound on her head like a crown. She wore canary-yellow slacks with a matching jacket, and her right hand was wrapped tightly around a man's hand.

''We're the Fontaines, John and Lily,'' the man told Anne, ''and this is our honeymoon.''

John Fontaine wasn't much bigger than his wife. He had the same black hair and deep-set brown eyes. A pair of powerful and expensive binoculars hung around his neck, and two plump, square cushions were wedged under his left arm.

"Congratulations," Anne said. "That's very romantic."

Lily laughed. "Isn't it?"

"Married yesterday in Nevada, but Lily has always wanted to go on a sailboat and see a whale," John explained.

"I grew up in Montana," Lily said. "I can't believe how beautiful the ocean is. John said we'll go to Hawaii when we get back from this trip. He has a house on Maui, and he says I won't believe the color of the water."

"*We* have a house on Maui," John corrected softly.

"I bet it's gorgeous," Anne told them.

"It'll be prettier when I get Lily over there," John said and was rewarded with a sparkling smile from his new wife. He pulled a brochure out of the inner pocket of his black windbreaker and flipped through it while the wind attempted to tear it from his fingers.

"Is that for this trip?" Anne asked.

"Yes, haven't you seen one?"

Anne admitted she hadn't.

"Give her that one, honey," Lily said. "We have another in our cabin."

John refolded it and insisted Anne take it. She put it in her rear pocket. "I guess I'd better get back to the kitchen—er, galley—" she said, and added, she hoped nonchalantly, "Oh, I hope you like gazpacho."

"We like everything," John insisted.

"How nice. Well, I'll see you guys later. Enjoy your afternoon."

"Oh, we're going to," Lily said, another dazzling smile breaking across her face. "John found a little spot on top of that forward cabin there at the bow where we can sit and watch the ocean. Maybe we'll be the first to spot a gray whale!''

"Good luck," Anne called.

She paused before going below decks. She told herself it was to watch the sails rise up the masts and feel the boat come alive as the engines were shut off and the world became a place of water and wind. But she also wanted one last look at Dave, his dark hair flying. She got her last look, but it also included Irene, who stood in front of Dave, her hands on the wheel too. A look of fierce concentration narrowed Irene's eyes as she attempted to keep the *Serenity* on course. Or did the look come from the fact that the handsome crewman had his hands over hers?

The wind caught the boat on a port tack and tipped her port rail toward the water. Anne heard several giggles as the passengers readjusted their balance and positions. She herself gripped the sides of the hatchway.

"This is great!" Irene said, laughing.

Anne descended the ladder and slipped on the second step. She wasn't looking where she was going and plowed right into Captain Bloom.

"Young woman!" he said softly, but his whisper was as good as another's bellow. "If I'd been one of the passengers, you'd have knocked me on my ear. You are to take care in the future, do you understand?"

"Yes, sir."

"Don't look so confounded devastated by a simple reprimand," he said sternly. He shook his head in disgust and climbed the ladder.

Anne retreated to the galley. She felt hot tears in her eyes—so silly—but she couldn't help it. The captain hated her. If he even suspected they were related, he'd probably have her thrown to the sharks. Well, she had two weeks to see to that. She wiped the tears away, determined to get her emotions under control.

She saw that Quince had put a pot of coffee on the stove, securing it with stainless-steel bars so that it didn't slide around as the boat climbed the small off-shore waves. She guessed that she should have thought of that herself. The colored mugs swung on their hooks. Well, she'd make coffee from now on, and she'd concentrate on Captain Bloom. If Rex Collier, her private eye, had been right, then her future might be linked with Samuel Bloom's future. Or maybe she'd decide to let the whole issue die. She wasn't sure that she wanted him in her future or that he'd want to be there even if what she expected was true. And if it was, if he was who she thought he was, it explained a lot about what had happened to her mother, Serena, so many years before.

Meanwhile there was a cake to bake, gazpacho to figure out. Anne tied her apron around her waist and began hunting for a cake pan.

Chapter Four

"I see one! I see a whale!"

Anne heard the excited declaration through her open porthole. She glanced at her watch. The cake was due out of the oven in five minutes. She raced toward the salon and up the ladder.

Lily and John Fontaine were still on the bow of the boat. The big foresails arched out over the ocean to their left. Lily was jumping as much as the precarious tilt of the boat allowed and was pointing toward the ocean.

"There!" Lily screamed. "See?"

Anne steadied herself by grasping an aft lifeline stanchion. She saw a disturbance ruffle the surface of the sea, an expanse of mottled gray skin, and a spray of water, and then heard the intake of breath that sounded like a vacuum cleaner switched on and off. Too soon, the whale's back (she assumed) rolled beneath the ocean and was gone.

She glanced at the foredeck. All the guests, Skip, Quince, and Samuel Bloom were looking beyond the first sighting, binoculars in hand, waiting for the whale to resurface.

"What do you think?" Dave asked. Irene had gone forward to get a good look at the whale, and he was alone at the wheel.

35

"It's wonderful, isn't it?" Anne said. "Just think, we're only a few hundred feet away from a whale."

"About thirty tons of *Eschrichtius robustus*, to be exact," he said with a grin.

"I gather that's Latin for gray whale?"

"Yep."

"How do you know it's a gray whale and not one of the other varieties?"

"It didn't have a dorsal fin," he explained. Another whale rolled against the top of the ocean and shot water to the sky to clear his blowhole before breathing. "Wait till we get to Mexico," he added. "Wait till you see them swimming under the boat and cavorting with their young."

"This is still exciting," Anne said.

"I know."

Their eyes met. It was several seconds before she remembered the cake. "Oh, dear," she said and quickly went back down the ladder, through the engine room, and into the galley.

"I can't believe it," Lily Fontaine said.

Anne smiled, pleased with the new bride's pleasure. The chocolate cake—lopsided, a tad burned—nevertheless announced *Serenity's* congratulations to the newlyweds.

"Very nice," Captain Bloom said. "Lily, will you do us the honor of cutting the cake?"

Anne felt an absurd rush of pleasure at the captain's compliment, delivered as briskly as always and without so much as a glance in her direction. She backed out of the salon, but not before her eyes met Dave's eyes. He was seated to the captain's right, but between the two men sat Irene, resplendent in pink silk, her hair a fair halo around her lovely face. Who in the world brought silk aboard a sailboat? Anne thought of how she herself must look: hair hanging in short, limp tendrils beside a flushed face, T-shirt and jeans covered with an apron that was in turn covered with chocolate frosting. Well, if Dave went for a pretty face, open adoration, and groomed hair, Anne was out of the running before she was in.

All the guests had dressed for dinner, except Patty, who was feeling sick and had decided to skip dinner. Without his wife's restraint, Boris was busy flirting with Irene, Liz, and even the new Mrs. Fontaine. The women looked amused, John Fontaine annoyed, and the male crew members of the *Serenity* oblivious.

It was dark outside, but the engines hadn't been turned on yet. Skip was behind the wheel, taking his watch. The rest of the crew were seated around the table with the guests on wooden chairs. Anne wondered where they'd gotten chairs. She went back to the galley and made a supper tray for Skip after she wedged the first set of dishes into the tiny sink to soak.

The cockpit was dark, illuminated only by a red light on the compass and the dim glow of the instrument panel. Anne knew the *Serenity* had radar aboard—she could see the round, white transmitter up in the smaller mizzenmast— and she knew the boat had an autopilot steering system because Quince had told her about it. She wondered why someone had to stay at the helm all the time if the instruments told it where to go and when another boat was close.

"Hungry?" she asked Skip.

"Always," he said. He spared a hand to grasp Anne's elbow as she stepped into the cockpit. The boat rose to a swell, and Anne half fell against Skip, her primary concern being that she didn't drop his dinner or spill his canned chicken soup.

"Sorry," she mumbled as she righted herself.

"I'm not," he said. "What's for dinner?"

"Fancy fish sandwiches. Don't grump at me—they were what Billy had planned, and I decided I'd better follow his menu, more or less, till I got the hang of this."

Skip took a hardy bite of the salad-filled croissant. "Captain always likes a light dinner first night aboard so the guests have a chance to get their sea legs before eating heavy food. This is good. Is that cake?"

"More or less. Is that the coastline?"

Skip nodded as he drank from the mug. Anne looked at the dark horizon. A few pinpoints of lights were all that defined the coast in this largely uninhabited section of California. The wind was cold and she shivered, but she felt reluctant to leave. The air smelled so fresh and clean; the stars were brilliant in the black sky; the wind was salty and moist. Even the sounds were unique—muted voices, sloshing water, sails flapping and slapping and rattling as the wind drove the sailboat through the night.

"It's lovely out here," she said, and in the back of her mind a vision of her store surfaced—dry, stuffy, cramped. Her Christmas boutique had been bought on a whim; it would be closed now for two weeks while she chased her dreams. "I thought the engines went on after dark," she added.

"Not tonight. Captain thought it best if everyone ate first. He always takes the eight-to-midnight watch so the guests can come out and talk to him while he steers and maybe try a hand themselves."

"He seems very concerned that they enjoy themselves."

Skip handed Anne the empty mug and picked up another sandwich. "Sure. Heck, there are plenty of whale-watching boats that take people out, buzz them up and down the coast, get them a lot closer to the whales than we can, and then deliver them home to their own beds in a matter of hours. What he sells on this boat is the atmosphere and the experience of being part of a small sailing ship.''

''Mm—'' Anne said. She closed her eyes for a second and tried to imagine being aboard as a guest, being waited on, free to lounge in the fresh air, read a book, work on a tan, look for a forty-foot whale. But the sinkload of dirty dishes down below kept getting in the way of this pleasant image.

''Is Mrs. Hygrade feeling better?'' Skip asked.

''Mrs. Hygrade?''

''Funny old lady with red hair like mine.''

''Oh, Boris's wife, Patty.'' Anne smiled. Patty's particular shade of red hair would be a complete surprise to Mother Nature. ''She was still in her cabin when I left.''

''She threw up earlier,'' Skip confided. ''All over the deck. Poor thing. She was greener than her coat.''

''I'll check on her,'' Anne said. ''What cabin are she and Boris in?''

''Stateroom 2. The two knockouts are sharing Number 1, and the Fontaines are in 3.''

''You noticed Irene, huh?''

''Irene?''

''The blond bombshell.''

He grinned sheepishly. ''Oh. I was thinking of the other one.''

Anne smiled to herself. ''Well, I'll look in on Patty Hygrade and see if she needs anything.''

''Thanks. She's really not so bad. Seems quite taken with the captain.''

''You sound very fond of the captain.''

''Sure I am. He's okay. You know where you stand with him, that's for sure.''

Anne didn't say anything, but she didn't agree with that last sentence, at least not yet. She had no idea where she stood with the man. But she did decide that she might be able to elicit a piece or two of information out of Skip, so she lingered a moment and asked, "Does the captain have any children?"

"He doesn't talk about family," he said around a mouthful of cake.

"Didn't he have a son?" she persisted.

"Where'd you hear that?"

Anne shrugged. "I'm not sure."

"Probably Quince or maybe Dave. Anyway, I think you're right. I think I remember hearing he had a son who died when he was a kid. That would be over twenty years ago now. Why are you asking about the captain's family?"

Anne shrugged. "Just curious." She waited for him to volunteer more information, but as none was forthcoming, she excused herself, begging galley duties. Thanks to Rex Collier, she already knew Samuel Bloom's son had died. He hadn't found out exactly how, so Anne was in the dark about that, but it was mind-boggling to think Skip might be referring in such an offhand way to her very own father.

Skip called after her. "You can take the tray. I'm all done except for the cake, and I don't need a tray for that. Any hot coffee down there?"

"I'll send up a cup."

"Great. Three cubes of sugar. And another piece of cake if there is any. It tastes different."

"It's burned," Anne admitted.

"I like it," Skip said.

She nodded her thanks but was becoming convinced that Skip liked anything with a high-enough sugar content.

It was almost midnight by the time Anne closed her cabin door behind her. There was still her suitcase to unpack, and Quince had just informed her that someone would wake her by six so she could get a head start baking bread for breakfast. She refused to even think about it. Without a recipe, the chances she could produce a loaf of bread aboard this boat were between zero and nothing.

As promised, she'd tried to look in on Patty Hygrade before cleaning the galley, but Boris had stopped her at their door. "She's asleep," he'd informed Anne. "I told the fool woman to take some seasick medicine, but she wouldn't. I'm just about to go up on deck and take watch with the captain." He lowered his voice and managed to rub his arm against Anne's arm. "Lots of pretty stars up there. Why don't you come along?"

"I have work to do," Anne had said quickly. "Good night." She laughed to herself, wondering if Boris kept taking his wife on ocean cruises because she was cabinbound with seasickness, allowing him the freedom to flirt outrageously.

She took the rest of her clothes out of the suitcase and stuffed them indiscriminately into drawers. She put all her toiletries into her makeup bag, which was by luck and not design large enough to hold everything, and put it in the head. Last thing out was a snapshot of her mother and stepfather, which she laid in the top drawer with her underwear, pausing for a moment to stare at it.

Serena and Ben Moore looked happy in the photo. No reason why they shouldn't. It had been taken in Paris, where they had gone for their seventeenth anniversary, only a month before a drunk driver made sure they'd never have another one. Anne had been told as a small child that Ben Moore wasn't her "real" father, but the words hadn't meant anything to her. Wasn't he there to help her build birdhouses and to read bedtime stories to her? And later, as she'd grown, he'd been the one to question boys when they came to the house, the one to scold her for the occasional bad grade. If that wasn't "real," what was? She'd never felt the need to know this mythical "real" father.

And then suddenly she was alone. The inheritance bought her the Christmas boutique, but it couldn't buy back her family, and for the first time she'd started wondering about the possibility of another family, another father. The wondering became longing as one lead after another petered out.

First she'd found a few papers in with her mother's belongings. Unfortunately they'd shed no precious facts about her biological father's identity, but she had discovered the name of the town in which her mother had briefly attended high school, and that had formed the starting point.

Her mother's parents were both long since gone, so they couldn't help. Eventually she'd found Rex Collier's name in the phone book and paid him his first advance to start investigating her mother's past. That was when she realized how little she knew about her mother's life before she met and married Ben Moore.

In the last two years the private investigator had dug up three names. The first two had petered out upon closer scrutiny. The last name was Ronald Bloom, son of Samuel Bloom. Ronald was dead, and so was the chance of a father. But maybe Samuel Bloom was her grandfather.

Only, how did she find out? It was no easier to ask him now that she was aboard his ship than it had been back at the dock. It was obviously going to take more than a few hours to get him to warm up to her. She knew Ronald had gone to school with her mother. What she needed to find out was how well he'd known her. In other words, had they been in love? Was the handwriting in the one letter Anne's mother had kept through the years his?

She opened the old envelope carefully and took out the much-folded piece of lined white paper within. The letter was short, and she knew it by heart, but she read it aloud, anyway.

My Serenity, I let you down last night when you needed me most. I was just so scared. You know my father— you know what he's like. He's had my future planned for me since I was ten years old, and it doesn't include a wife and a kid before college. I know your parents didn't plan this for you, either, but at least they're reasonable people. Dad is—well, you know what Dad is. Anyway, I'll tell him, I promise, but not until after graduation. I just can't take that away from him. I love you, Serena, and I will try to be the serenity for you that you've always been for me. Everything will work out, I promise. R.

The letter was dated seven months before Anne's birth. "R" had never married her mother. A year later Serena had married Ben Moore, and Anne liked to think she'd never looked back.

So, R was her biological father, but who was he? What facts did she have? Her mother was a junior in high school at the time, and this R must have been a year older, hence the talk about graduation. The R was either the beginning letter of the first name, the last name, or a nickname. Of the thirty graduating senior boys, only one last name began with an R, and he was Asian. Anne was obviously not half Asian, but she'd had Collier check him out, anyway. Dead end. Three senior boys' names began with the letter R. Collier had investigated and subsequently ruled out the first two. Ronald Bloom was the third. So that left Ronald Bloom, but he had died in a boating accident the summer after high-school graduation.

If it wasn't Ronald Bloom, then the R must have stood for a nickname or been the initial of a boy from church or down the block. It didn't matter. She didn't have the resources or the information to dig deeper. This was her last chance.

What a wealth of hogwash this would all sound like to Samuel Bloom! She had to ask more questions, try to narrow things down before she spoke to him. He wasn't the kind of man with whom to have a cozy chat. She'd have to pump Quince and maybe Dave. But she'd have to be careful and not arouse their curiosity. Because even if she was right, even if Samuel Bloom was her grandfather, that didn't mean he would be thrilled about it or want to claim her.

On the other hand, had his son had something to do with naming this boat the *Serenity*? Wasn't that quite a coincidence?

And on the other-other hand—if, indeed, there was such a thing—there was no denying that she longed for it all to be true. Surely, eventually, she'd start to grow on the captain. And as brusque as he was, she already suspected she rather liked him. She didn't think it would take too much of a shove to actually love the crusty old seadog.

If it was true. If he was her grandfather. And if he wasn't, she was at the end of the line and alone.

Chapter Five

Anne gave up trying to sleep at two-thirty A.M. She could hear the dull throb of the engines driving the boat on, but the sea was big enough to make the ride uncomfortable, and the smell of the diesel fuel that seeped through the bulkhead didn't help matters. She turned on the little light above her bed and looked at the teak ceiling.

Finally she reached for the brochure John Fontaine had given her the afternoon before that she'd been too tired to read. The cover was decorated with a beautiful picture of the *Serenity* under sail along with the words, *Come Sail the Serenity*! emblazoned across the mainsail in vibrant yellow.

She opened the brochure and found out when the ship departed—yesterday—and when it was due to arrive back in port. She found out that the guests had the option of going ashore the next day—no, make that today—for a private tour of Hearst Castle, the mansion that newspaper tycoon William Randolph Hearst had spent over thirty years building and that was now part of the California Park system. It sat up in the hills overlooking San Simeon Bay, surveying the Pacific Ocean in opulent splendor. That night—tonight!—there was to be a "Fantastic Barbecue" aboard the ship, and the next morning they'd depart for the Channel Islands off the California coast.

Come feel the adventure of years gone by, the brochure tempted. *Private staterooms, delightful cuisine, shore day trips, San Ignacio Lagoon, and, of course, your companions in the southerly trek—the California gray whales. See them without endangering them or yourself or interrupting the grand design of Mother Nature as the Serenity shares the sea with her creatures, both large and small.*

The brochure promised added adventures, but Anne put it aside. Reading while the boat pounded and rocked had been a mistake. She sat up, suddenly dizzy, her stomach lurching in protest. She pulled her coat on over her sweatpants and T-shirt and let herself into the galley.

A dim light burned on the bulkhead. The boat was dark and silent, except for the engine. The coffeepot was on the stove, doubtlessly fortifying the lucky stiff on watch. Anne climbed the ladder and slid back the main hatch.

"Hey, you're ruining my night vision!" barked a dark shape hovering in the cockpit behind the wheel.

Anne recognized Dave's voice, but her only thought was making it to the rail before getting sick. "Sorry," she mumbled as she slid the hatch closed and collapsed on a seat.

"Anne? What are you doing awake?"

Trying not to throw up, she thought as she gulped fresh air. "Couldn't sleep," she said.

"You should be wearing a harness. Didn't anyone tell you that?"

She looked at him, or at as least as much as was visible in the only light that came from the engine controls and the red compass light. "No," she said.

"Safety rule number one. Do not come out on deck at night without putting on a safety harness and clipping the line to the safety line that runs amidship. I can't believe no one told you about it.''

Anne shrugged. She had the lurking suspicion the captain hoped she'd fall overboard and he'd be rid of her. "Things happened a little fast," she told him. "Where are these safety harnesses?"

"Right by the main hatch."

"Next time," she promised.

"No, not next time. Now."

"Dave—"

"Don't argue, Anne."

By now her stomach was settling back where it belonged. The thought of going back inside. . . . "How can I go get one without destroying your night vision again?" she groaned.

"Just do it. I'll avert my eyes."

Anne sighed. She stood as the boat tumbled sideways and tossed her against the free-standing brass binnacle. "Need to get my sea legs," she muttered as she went back inside. Sure enough, several maroon harnesses hung in the coat locker to the starboard side of the ladder. She fished one out, snapped it over her coat as fast as she could, and went back outside once again, careful to close the hatch behind her.

"The line is off to your left," he said. "Just clip the free end of the tether to the line."

"Yes, sir," Anne said as she did as directed. "Now that I can't fall overboard, may I please sit down?"

"Of course."

She settled back against the seat, hugging her coat close for warmth.

They lapsed into silence. Anne looked toward the shore. It appeared the boat was getting closer to land, but the ocean and the coast looked almost the same, and she was no judge of distances at sea. Besides, she didn't really care. Now that she was outside, she felt better, and the idea of sleep fled from her mind.

"Tell me all about yourself," Dave said. "Every little detail."

She looked up at his face, heavily shadowed, only the twinkle of his eye glimmering in the night. "There's nothing much to tell," she said.

"Oh, come on. What were you before you decided to run away to sea?"

"A shopkeeper."

"What kind of shop and where?"

"A Christmas boutique in Seattle, Washington."

"Christmas boutique? What in the world is a Christmas boutique?"

She laughed. "It's a store that sells artsy-craftsy little Christmas-type things all year long."

"All year round? You're kidding."

"Nope. I could hardly believe it myself. My parents died in an automobile accident, and the drunk driver who killed them was uninsured, so I inherited very little money. I was also twenty and kind of . . . lost. I quit college when I saw this little shop was for sale. I bought it kind of on impulse."

"Pardon me for saying so, but wasn't that kind of a weird acquisition for a twenty-year-old?"

Anne shrugged. "I was . . . desolate. Like I said, at the time I was short on money and dreams . . . it was kind of like I was in limbo. I saw a sign in the window of this small shop and went inside. You should have seen it. Everything was shiny and bright and . . . hopeful. That sounds stupid."

"No, it doesn't," he said softly.

"The owner wanted out. At the time I couldn't imagine why she was willing to carry the papers or sell it to me for a song. Now, of course, I realize she was sick and tired of

Christmas. She was fed up with bells and holly and wreaths and crystal snowflakes. She was at the end of her rope with reindeer, Santa Claus, cinnamon sticks, and Styrofoam snowmen. She probably felt as though she'd like to swat the next person who said 'Merry Christmas' in April, to say nothing of what she'd like to do to the people who bragged they'd completed their Christmas shopping by June. I walked into that shop on July third, and by July seventh I was the new proprietor. I hear the old owner moved to Hawaii and opened a shop that sells grass mats and suntan lotion. She was just at the end of her rope.''

Dave laughed. ''She doesn't sound like the only one.''

''Yeah, I guess I am too. I'm sorry, I usually don't whine to strangers.''

''Oh? Who do you whine to?''

She laughed. ''I whine internally. Externally I am cheerful and reliable. Most of the time.''

''No special man to listen to your woes?''

She looked toward him. What she wouldn't have given for a flashlight! ''No,'' she said smoothly.

''Hm— What I really want to know is, do you still enjoy Christmas?''

''Not much.'' Actually, she didn't blame the shop alone for that. It was simply that most holidays had ceased to have much meaning. The first year she was alone, she'd tackled a turkey and invited friends, and they'd come, sympathetic to her loss. But all during dinner she'd had the feeling they couldn't wait to be with their own families, and the second year she'd gone it alone with a rented movie. Aloud, she said, ''The boutique gave me direction when I didn't have any. Besides, February is real slow, so I get to take two weeks off and goof around as long as I can find a way to do it on a budget.''

''And this is your idea of goofing around?'' he asked.

"Sure," she said and was relieved when he let the issue drop.

After a moment he asked, "Are those your teeth clattering together, or are you playing the castanets?"

"I'm playing the castanets," she told him. "I've got a whole band over here. Maracas, marimbas, the whole works."

"That's what I figured. Get up and look inside that locker you're sitting on. You should find a wool blanket or two. Wrap one around yourself."

She opened the locker, but it was too dark to see anything. Her fingers felt wool, and she pulled a dark blanket from the locker. It was a lot warmer when she had this firmly wrapped around her legs.

"Aren't you cold?" she asked.

"I wear long underwear."

"Sounds smart." She looked at him again and saw the flash of his teeth as he smiled. "It's your turn. Tell me about you."

"Well, as you so acutely observed, I'm smart. I'm also strong, good-looking, kind, dependable—"

"A regular Boy Scout?"

"That's right. Move your legs to the side, will you? I can't see the oil-pressure gauge. Thanks. Where was I?"

"Dependable—"

"Oh, yeah. A regular prince of a fellow."

"Where were you when your car broke down?"

"Oh, that. Colorado, visiting my mother. I got it stuck in an eight-foot snowbank. Thank goodness I don't live in that kind of weather anymore. Give me warm water and a sailboat."

"Do you sail on this boat all year long?"

"For the last year I have. Summer in Alaska in the inland passage or across to Hawaii, winter in the Bahamas, a once-a-year spring trip to the California coast—here and there, a sailing nomad.''

"And do you love it?''

"Yes,'' he said simply. "I do.'' He paused and Anne felt the boat lift to a large swell and roll down the back side. He added, "I love it out here. I love the smells and the sounds and the stars overhead. I love having my hands on the wheel, love feeling the boat churn her way through the sea, even when the iron sails are in charge.''

"Iron sails?''

"The engine,'' he said, laughing. "Have you sailed much before this?''

"Not much. A little on Puget Sound when I was younger. My . . . my father had a small sailboat, and we'd go tinker around on a summer day.''

"It sounds like fun.''

"It was,'' she said, remembering those long-gone days with fondness.

"I envy you,'' he remarked. "Maybe you lost your dad, but at least you knew him.''

It was on the tip of her tongue to tell Dave that Ben Moore wasn't her real father. But she saw Ben's face creased in smiles as the wind filled their small sails and heard his voice telling her to haul in the jib sheet, and it seemed disloyal to even think of him in those terms. He had been her real father in every way that counted. If the longing for a family would just go away, she'd be happy to let the whole issue drop.

"Listen to the night,'' Dave said softly. "Sometimes when I'm out here alone on night watch, I think about the water beneath me and the vast stretch of ocean before and behind—it makes a man feel small. Not in a negative sense, but more like he's a leaf on a tree, a part of something bigger and better than he can ever see.''

"Leaves turn brown and fall to the ground," she said.

"Eventually. And then new ones spring up and the old ones form mulch— This conversation is getting pretty philosophical for the middle of the night."

Anne smiled to herself. She remembered her first nervous reaction to him, only a short fourteen hours before. The impact of his confidence and self-reliance still lingered in her mind, reinforced by the simple conviction of his words and tone of his voice. She also remembered the fluttering awareness that had gnawed at her stomach—awareness of him as a man, an awareness sharpened by his appearance and something that shined in his eyes. She was infatuated with him, and the fact that she didn't really know him yet seemed a minor detail. A bigger inconvenience was the fact that he lived aboard the *Serenity*, wandered here and there, and probably wanted a woman loving him about as much as Samuel Bloom wanted a long-lost granddaughter.

"I'm sorry about your parents," he said suddenly.

"Thank you," Anne said. "Losing them was . . . devastating. It happened so quickly." For a second she relived the police visit, the identification of their bodies, going home alone when it was over. "We were close," she explained. "I think that makes it worse." It had been two years, and she still wasn't used to the finality of the whole thing. Maybe that was what drove her so hard to replace them—as if that were possible.

"I think I understand how you feel," Dave said. "My dad died when I was four. When I was in high school, my best friend's dad used to love to take him fishing and camping. Jay hated all that stuff. I used to be green with envy."

"I thought you were speaking metaphorically before, that you'd grown up with your father but never knew him. Do you remember him at all?"

"Not much. He was tall—well, at least to me—and he

carried me around on his shoulders. It's hard to tell how much I really remember about him and how much I've gathered from stories and old photographs.''

"You'll have your own son someday," she said softly. "You can take him camping and fishing."

"Yes." Then he added, "He'll probably be like Jay and won't go with me." He fumbled with some electronic controls, then sat down on the seat next to her. "I put the boat on auto pilot," he said.

"I was wondering about that," she told him. "I mean, if the boat can steer herself and you have radar to know when someone else is approaching, then why does someone have to stay out here all the time?"

"Because we're so close to the coast and shipping lanes. And while we may look big to us, we're not even a bleep on a radar screen to one of those oil supertankers. You're still cold."

"A little," she admitted, but the truth of the matter was that the present shivering had nothing to do with the cold and everything to do with Dave's proximity.

He put his arm around her shoulders. "Do you mind if I do my best to keep the new cook warm?" he asked.

She looked up at his face. She could see the shadowed wells above his cheekbones and the glimmer that shone from his eyes. "No." The sound of the engine covered the shaking in her voice.

"Look at the sky," he said. "The moon is wearing a halo tonight."

Anne did as directed. The moon was waxing and still had a week before it would be full. The sky was covered with a high ceiling of clouds, invisible except around the moon where the light refracted and made the shallow halo Dave mentioned. His arm tightened around her shoulders, and she felt his free hand touch her face. She looked at him and returned his smile; then his lips touched hers.

"Couldn't help myself," he said afterward. "Salt air, brisk wind, a beautiful companion—a kiss seemed kind of mandated."

Anne laughed as though easy flirtation were something she was used to. Her lips burned where he'd touched them with his, and she was tempted to initiate another, longer kiss.

" 'Course, there's the added complication that I've wanted to kiss you ever since I first saw you. You believe in love at first sight?"

She laughed again and didn't answer.

"Me too," he said and rested his head against hers.

She was baffled, intrigued, heady with romance, excited. Gradually all these feelings softened, dimmed. The steady throb of the engines and the warmth from Dave's body combined to send her thoughts into a hazy swirl that called her deeper and deeper into sleep.

The next thing Anne knew, Quince was shaking her shoulder. "It's after six, Missy," he said around the pipe stem.

She sat up abruptly. The gray wool blanket fell around her feet. She'd been stretched out on the cockpit seat; her pillow looked suspiciously like Dave's sweater. She dimly recalled falling asleep against him, and a glow of warmth spread throughout her body.

"How long—"

"Don't know," Quince said. "Guess you came up here during Dave's watch. I took over at four o'clock, and Dave said to let you sleep, that you got sick in your own cabin. Is that true?"

She started to lie and say that it wasn't, but the glint of

amusement in Quince's eyes told her there was no reason to pretend. "A little," she admitted.

"Thought so. Well, don't you worry. I won't tell the captain. Now, you'd better get your tail down below and get a hot shower before the paying guests want their share of the water. You know how to conserve fresh water?"

"I suppose it's just like camping. Get wet, turn it off, lather, rinse?"

"You got it."

Anne nodded. As she stood, she realized she was still tethered to the boat. She unclipped the harness and finally noticed that the boat was rocking gently, but not moving forward any longer, and that the engine was off. She looked around and found *Serenity* anchored in a beautiful little bay. Had she actually managed to sleep while the anchor was lowered?

"San Simeon," Quince said between puffs.

"It's beautiful," Anne said. The bay was surrounded with rolling green mountains and a sandy beach. Reluctantly she turned her back on the view and went below to take a shower.

An hour later, covered with flour, Anne looked at her biscuit dough. It wasn't exactly bread, but without a recipe, it was as close to a bread product as she was going to get. She rolled the dough and cut the biscuits. Billy's menu included cantaloupe halves filled with strawberries, scrambled eggs, and canned bacon. She downed another seasick pill to fight the woozy, achy feeling, opened both ports to get some air in the galley, and started washing the dishes in preparation for cooking breakfast.

In the back of her mind she worked on the questions she'd ask the captain when she got him alone. He'd probably stay aboard today while the guests toured Hearst Castle. Maybe if she talked to him about her family, he'd mention his. She needed to know if he remembered any of his son's friends, if Ron had ever mentioned her mother's name. Who knows? Maybe Ron had admitted Serena was pregnant and the old man had spent his life wondering what had become of his grandchild, of her, and had named his boat after the young woman his youngest son loved.

It was almost eleven by the time everyone had bathed, eaten, and gathered on deck for the ride to the beach. Dave and Skip had inflated one of the orange Zodiac rafts and attached a small outboard to the transom. It floated there now, tied to the *Serenity,* its bow thumping against the bigger ship as the Pacific Ocean rolled into the bay.

"Is everyone going?" Anne asked Quince. Captain Bloom had a camera slung over his shoulder.

"The captain and all the guests are. Me and Dave are going to stay here and work on the fore hatch. She took a little water last night."

Anne nodded. Well, at least she wouldn't have to fix a fancy lunch, but another opportunity for investigation was slipping away. Her eyes met Irene's eyes. Today the beautiful blonde was wearing white linen—a fabric Anne had never dared touch on dry land, let alone on the sea—and she looked cool, sophisticated, and slightly bored. Dave helped her down the ladder into the dinghy, where Skip took her hand till she was sitting next to Liz.

"Skip will stay with the dinghy on the beach," Quince said.

"How will everyone get to the castle?" Anne asked as she looked at the grandiose structure nestled high in the mountains.

"Previous arrangement for a private tour. See that green van? It'll take the folks up the hill. They'll eat lunch there, tour the grounds and the house, then return late this afternoon. Look there at Patty. The woman can barely wait to get into that dinghy and get her feet back on dry ground.''

"She's been fighting seasickness," Anne told him.

Quince shook his head and puffed on his pipe, the idea of being sick on the sea about as alien to him as the idea of being sick on land was to Anne.

The day stayed clear and sunny. Anne glanced at the menu and saw that Billy had planned something called "dutchess potatoes" to go with the steak. She clicked her tongue and decided on twice baked—at least she knew what they were. She also got a head start on the huge tossed green salad. She found a plastic bag of washed lettuce greens in the refrigerator, full of at least three different kinds of lettuce. She also found a bag full of crisp raw onion rings, a tomato, and a bottle of homemade vinaigrette dressing.

While digging in the fridge, she also unearthed a plastic container full of tomato soup that smelled wonderful thanks to onions and garlic. Billy had obviously done a lot of food preparation for this trip. She thought that if she were the captain, she wouldn't have fired him as long as he could walk.

What was she going to do once all Billy's careful menu ideas were gone? She'd have to restock the food, decide every meal down to the salad, be sure not to use something for lunch one day that was needed for dinner the next. It was a daunting thought, but she was determined not to fail. Samuel Bloom had told her he didn't think she was up to the challenge. One way or another she'd prove to him she was. If she was soon to announce herself as his granddaughter, it would be nice if he could stand the sight of her.

She washed out the dish towels and decided to take advantage of the sun outside to dry them. Somewhere in the galley she'd spotted a small bag of wooden clothespins. She found them and carried everything up on deck.

Dave and Quince were on the foredeck. Quince was surrounded by his usual cloud of bluish pipe smoke, but Dave had taken off his shirt while he worked. Anne spent an idle moment watching his muscles ripple under his skin as he sanded and drilled the wood. She looked away before they caught her spying, and she started hanging the cloths on the line to dry in the breeze.

It was while she was searching on the cockpit floor for a lost clothespin that she looked up and noticed the radar spinning slowly around in its perch above the mizzenmast spreaders.

"Is this thing supposed to be on?" she called to Dave. She pointed high, and both men's gazes followed her lead.

"Nope," Quince hollered. "You want to turn it off, Missy? Our hands are kind of full."

Anne nodded. "Sure." She gathered up the last clothespins and put them back into their plastic bag, then went down inside. It was the first time she'd entered the starboard passageway that led first to navigation, then to the captain's quarters, and she felt as though she were trespassing.

The navigation center consisted of a whole bank of machines set secured to a bulkhead. Rolled-up charts were tucked into a wooden frame above her head. Instruments were behind another grill-worked cabinet door, and a large work space and bench were beneath. One machine had a bright-green screen like a small television. Anne could discern a map of the San Simeon Bay. Brighter green glitches blinked here and there. Anne saw the on/off switch and flipped it, and the map faded away as the screen went dark.

The captain's stateroom door was ajar. Anne turned away from it and then stopped. Would his walls be covered with photographs the way Quince's were? She looked toward the ladder, was reassured by the silence, and gently pushed the door open.

The cabin was all varnished mahogany. The small built-in bunk was wider than the one Anne slept in and was covered with a deep-green spread. The whole cabin was neat and clean, almost austere. The walls were blank except for two photographs hung above the small desk.

Serenity's picture, the same one as in the brochure, was the biggest. The other picture was of a family. A woman and man stood to the sides of two young men, one about twelve, the other closer to twenty. It wasn't hard to pick out a younger Samuel Bloom, obviously the father. The same square jaw and uncompromising glare confronted the camera. The woman was younger, darker, happier looking. The boys seemed to favor her coloring and temperament.

Anne looked closer at the boys. They were obviously related, but it wasn't the implied fact she might have an uncle somewhere that held her gaze. For the first time she saw something familiar in their faces, and she felt her heart race. Her fingers, of their own volition, reached up to touch the glass, to touch the faces of both boys one by one. Frozen in time, they smiled at her. Which one? It would have to be the younger.

Oh, he was handsome in his young, innocent way. Younger than she was now, she realized. His smile said his whole life was ahead of him, unknowing it would be snatched away prematurely. ''Father?'' she whispered.

''Anne?''

She jerked and dropped her hand, whirling to face Dave. He'd pulled on a shirt. Speckles of white paint glittered on his arms.

''I . . .'' she began and then faltered. There was no excuse for being in the captain's cabin, and they both knew it.

He nodded, a smile softening his look. ''I wouldn't let *him* catch you in here,'' he said at last.

"No," she agreed and walked past him, too embarrassed to meet his eyes.

Some furious activity in the galley helped Anne work out the jumble of feelings that churned her insides. Foremost was the growing conviction that she was right—the captain was her grandfather. Warmth and thrill seeped into her heart in equal measures. Samuel Bloom wasn't nurturing like Ben Moore, or funny or kindhearted. But she didn't care. It was enough to find a link, to know he was hers in a private, intimate way. She could love him and maybe thaw him, and in the future maybe he would love her and want her as part of his life. And there was also the distinct possibility of an uncle and maybe cousins.

Eventually Anne walked down the long deck, steaming mugs of tomato soup and a tray of sandwiches and cold glasses of milk in her hands. She avoided Dave's eyes, though she could feel him watching her.

"Lunch break," she said.

Quince took one look at the sandwiches and shook his head. "Is that peanut butter?"

"Yes."

"Heck, girl, I don't eat peanut butter."

"Well, there's one salmon-filled croissant left in the fridge. I'll run back and get it for—"

"No, no. You kids eat your lunch. I'll go get my own sandwich and eat it inside out of the sun."

He tapped the bowl of his pipe against a life stanchion and sauntered back toward the cabin.

"I like peanut butter," Dave said. He was running a rag up and down his tanned arms, cleaning off the paint. His gaze met Anne's.

She was wondering what she should say about being caught in the captain's cabin, but a quick smile from Dave convinced her that it was better to let the whole thing drop.

She sat down beside him. "I had this feeling you did."
He took a bite and looked curious.

"You just seem like the peanut-butter type," she explained.

"Oh? You don't think of me as the moussaka type?"

She laughed. "I have no idea what the moussaka type is, do you?"

"Nope. And you're right, I do like peanut butter. But I also like fancy gourmet food. In fact, first night ashore when you don't have to cater to the passengers, I'll buy you dinner in an expensive restaurant and redeem myself in your eyes."

"Not necessary. I adore peanut butter."

"Is necessary," he assured her. "Anyway, an extravagant dinner is just a flimsy excuse for getting you alone. Is it a date?"

"If you want—"

"I want. I've never tasted gazpacho hot before," he added as he took a sip from the mug. "It's good this way."

Anne smiled. "Thanks." The mystery was solved—gazpacho was cold tomato soup. She closed her eyes. The sun felt good on her skin, Dave was close—who could want anything more? Wouldn't it be something if her desire for a family resulted in a grandfather and Dave, all in one trip?

"I shouldn't have kissed you last night," he said suddenly.

Anne narrowed her eyes against the sun and looked into his eyes. "Is that so?" she asked. "I rather enjoyed it."

She saw his smile ignite his eyes and felt her breath quicken. "I just don't want you to think I go around kissing indiscriminately," he said.

"Don't you?" she asked innocently.

"Oh, no. I choose the recipient of my kisses very carefully."

"Really?"

"I look for eyes the color of a tropical sea and hair like sun-kissed gold."

"You're a poet as well as a good kisser," she told him.

"I'm a romantic at heart," he agreed. "Don't tell me you're one of these ultramodern girls who doesn't believe in romance."

"I believe in romance," she said softly.

He looked into her eyes, deep into her eyes, and said, "I know. And this is going to sound insane, but, Anne, I felt something inside my heart kind of spring to life the first time I saw you."

"You're sure it wasn't the bananas swinging back and forth?"

"I'm sure," he said firmly. "You're forgetting I saw you out on the dock first, with Quince."

She looked down at the teak deck. It did sound insane, but she'd felt it too. "It's all happening too fast," she said cautiously.

He nodded. "Maybe you're right. Maybe it is. But I want you to know how I feel—that I think I'm— Okay, I won't say more." He lifted her chin with gentle fingers and kissed her, this time with a little more purpose.

Anne giggled softly when it was over. After all, she'd come to the *Serenity* in hopes of finding a family, and here was Dave, and all she could think about was him.

"My kisses are now making you laugh?"

"Yes," she said with shining eyes. "Isn't it wonderful?"

They both heard a discreet cough and looked up to find Quince advancing down the deck, his gaze directed toward the open ocean. "Looks like it might rain tonight," he called.

Anne gathered up the empty glasses and napkins, then stood. "It had better not rain till one of you barbecues those steaks," she said. She cast one last look at Dave and went below deck to wash lunch dishes and begin making the cheesecake Billy had decreed should be dessert. Luckily he'd bought a mix and a can of cherries so that her cooking talents wouldn't be stretched any further than they were already.

The guests were in good moods when they returned to *Serenity*. Patty confided to everyone that she'd finally decided to wear a seasick medicine patch behind her ear as Boris had told her to do all along and that she was finished hugging the commode! Even Irene returned Anne's smile.

Anne set the filet mignon steaks out on a platter while she put the previously prepared stuffed baked potatoes into the oven to heat them through and melt the cheese. She was tearing the greens into a bowl, listening to the captain entertain the guests while pouring them cocktails, when Quince came through the galley.

"Barbecue ready?" she asked.

"I think so. I'll get Sam's grandson to come down for the meat."

Anne closed the oven and stared at Quince. "The captain's grandson is aboard?"

He stole an avocado wedge from the salad. " 'Course, didn't you know that?"

Just then Samuel Bloom's voice bellowed from the main salon. "Quince? Come in here and tell Patty I wasn't lying about that incident with the Jamaican fellow. Quince!"

"Coming, coming," he said.

Anne caught his arm. "Aboard right now? When did he come aboard?" All she could think of was that a grandson meant a possible cousin. . . .

"Heaven's sake, Missy. He's been aboard the whole dadburned time. Dave is the captain's grandson. Don't tell

Sail Away!

me he didn't mention it to you this afternoon when he was
sweet-talking you?''

"He didn't mention it," she said woodenly.

"Well, neither one of them talks about it much. Dave's
too busy proving himself, and Sam—well, Sam is Sam."

"Quince!" the captain hollered.

Anne let go of Quince's arm and stood rooted to the cabin
sole. She felt like a suddenly deflated balloon, limp and
sick at heart. She'd managed to fall in love with a man who
might be her cousin, might even be her half brother.

"Oh, Dave," she mumbled.

Chapter Six

The rest of the evening passed in slow motion. As Anne served dinner, she watched everyone at the table but Dave. She saw Skip and Liz deep in conversation about sailing, Patty flirting with Samuel and Quince, Boris flirting with Irene and Lily Fontaine, who was completely oblivious of his attention, seeing as she only had eyes for her new husband. Quince had done the barbecuing, and she'd heard him tell Dave that they would stay at anchor till morning, when they'd get under way and head toward the Channel Islands, off the coast of Santa Barbara.

The blossoming feelings of love so intoxicating in the afternoon had turned to a cold lump of clay in Anne's chest. She knew she had to talk to Dave, to find out if he was Ron Bloom's son. And she had to talk to the captain too. She would just ask him about his son and about her mother. This stalling was only going to drive her crazy. On the other hand—there she went again—what if she was his granddaughter and Dave's cousin or half sister and they weren't happy about it? The *Serenity* was a large boat, but after all, only ninety feet. If the purpose was to avoid someone, ninety feet wasn't much room to maneuver in.

Dave. She peeked at him as she served slices of cheesecake dripping in cherries. Irene was sitting next to him, resplendent in aqua, her eyes brilliant in the warm glow of the kerosene lantern. Dave looked up, and Anne saw a tiny wink crinkle the corner of his left eye. His lips were ever so slightly curved, and he rested his chin in his palm. She looked down, but she could still feel his eyes on her. How was she going to live through the next twelve days?

"Have you ever been to Hearst Castle?" Lily asked.

Anne dropped the knife and watched as it sank into the cheesecake. Involuntarily she glanced at Samuel Bloom, who regarded her with an expression halfway between a scowl and a sneer.

She pulled the knife from the cheesecake and cut another slice. "No, I haven't," she said.

"Oh, it's beautiful," Lily gushed. "We're going to build an indoor pool at our new home, and I want it to look just like the Roman Pool."

"I guess I better open another department store," John said. "I suppose you want all that mosaic tile and the gold inlay too?" He grinned affectionately at his wife as he accepted a slice of cheesecake from Anne.

"Details," Lily said with a wave of her hand followed with a delightful peal of laughter. "But, Anne, I felt so bad you missed seeing the castle with us."

Anne handed a piece of cheesecake to Dave. His fingers touched hers, and she looked at him. His look said a million words, none of them appropriate between relatives.

"I loved the Antonio Canova sculpture," Liz said. She looked at Anne, her round face creased with intensity, and added, "It's called the 'Three Graces.' I think it's made out of white marble."

"The one of the three young girls embracing?" Irene asked Liz.

"Yes. I mean, all the sculptures were marvelous, and the

gardens were so beautiful . . . but that one piece looked so
. . . well, joyful!'' She glanced down at her hands and added,
''I guess that sounds dumb.''

''No, it doesn't,'' Irene said, her voice surprisingly soft.
''I thought the very same thing. And did you notice the
stained-glass windows? The colors glow like they're lit from
within.''

Anne smiled. She felt the captain's gaze on her and returned his stare. There was something odd in his eyes, some
sense of speculation lurking in the intense blue depths. She
turned away.

''You've been avoiding me,'' Dave said.

Anne was on the foredeck. She'd gone on deck after she
finished washing the dishes and was sitting on the bowsprit,
cradled in a folded sail on the jutting bowsprit. Down below,
Skip had opened a sliding door across from the table and
produced a small color television and VCR. Another concealed door revealed quite a selection of movies. When the
wind blew just right, Anne could hear the musical the guests
and the crew were enjoying.

Dave wedged himself in next to her and took her hand.
The spreader lights were on, shining down onto the deck
from their perch high upon the main mast. Anne could see
Dave's mouth, but a trick of lighting kept his eyes in
shadow. She had no doubt her entire face was illuminated.

''What's wrong?'' he asked.

''Nothing.''

He squeezed her hand. ''Dinner was delicious.''

''Thank you,'' she said formally as she slid her hand
from his grasp.

He looked startled by her withdrawal. ''I'm sorry,'' he
said. ''I guess I shouldn't have assumed. . . . Well, I'll
leave you alone.'' He started to stand.

Anne could barely stand being that close to him, but she also didn't want him to leave. She touched his arm, and he sank back down to the deck.

She dredged a smile from the bottom of her soul and said softly, "Dave, I like you, I really do. You're funny and gentle, and—well, I like you."

"Good."

"But you were right this afternoon. Things are going too fast."

"Actually," he said, "I believe you're the one who first mentioned that." When she didn't answer, he added, "You're afraid I'm an insincere sailor who puts the make on every pretty girl who passes by."

"No. Not that. But we don't know each other yet. Let's just talk for a while."

His lips parted, and the night air filled with his chuckle. "If you insist, but I have to warn you that I kiss better than I talk."

This time Anne's smile occurred spontaneously. "Maybe I was wrong about you. Maybe you do have a different woman in every port."

"Two, sometimes three," he said.

"And all pretty."

"Ravishing. Like you."

"Dave—"

"Okay. Okay. What do you want to talk about?"

"Anything. Your father. Your grandfather."

Now his mouth formed a small O. He paused for a moment, then he said, "I begin to see. Someone told you I'm the captain's grandson, right?"

"Quince mentioned it. Why the secret?"

He shrugged and repositioned his body so that his eyes came into the light. "Samuel Bloom is a complicated man. Like I told you last night, my father died when I was real little. He was out boating with his younger brother, Ronnie. Ronnie was waterskiing. He must have hit a submerged log because suddenly he went down. Dad went back for him. A woman on the shore saw Frank—that was my dad—dive into the lake after Ron. Neither one of them ever resurfaced. Pretty soon the boat drifted into shore, and a couple of days later divers pulled Ronnie and Frank from the lake.''

Anne wiped away tears. If Ron Bloom was her father, as she suspected he must be, then her father was responsible for Dave's father's death. An eerie feeling ran up her spine and down her arms. She felt the wound of their deaths as though it were fresh and raw. With an effort she mumbled, ''I'm . . . I'm sorry.''

Dave took a deep breath. ''My mother moved to Colorado to be with her family. She and Samuel Bloom didn't exactly see eye to eye on things, and there was no reason to stay in Washington State once Dad was gone. I don't think my grandfather ever forgave her for taking me away, though. His wife was long gone, and his sons were all he had. Anyway, after college I decided to look the old man up, and lo and behold, I actually liked him! He offered me a job aboard the *Serenity*, and I took it. Mother about died, of course. She thought a master's degree in business could be put to better use than fooling around on boats.''

''But your grandfather's blood runs deep in your veins,'' Anne said softly.

He smiled. ''Yes. That's what I like about you, Anne. You've known me all of thirty-three hours, and you know that already.''

''Because I've never seen you in another context,'' she pointed out. ''It's different for your mother.''

He nodded. ''Maybe so. But all I want is to get my Coast Guard chartering license and take over the *Serenity* when the captain retires.''

"Hard to imagine Samuel Bloom retiring," she said.

The old canvas sail crackled as Dave leaned back against it. "Yeah. Hard to see him raising cattle or farming, isn't it? But he's tough and, God willing, he won't give it up for years. There's plenty on the *Serenity* for all of us to do. Take that old blabbermouth, John Quincy Adams. No one knows their way around an engine like him. He's trying to teach me what he knows, but I'm a hopeless mechanic. I'd much rather fool around with the sails. You wouldn't believe the sail inventory the *Serenity* carries. There's a locker below where we're sitting, and it's stuffed with genoas, three spinnakers, a storm jib, this great beautiful red-and-white striped mizzen staysail— Well, I guess you get the point. But Quincy loves that blasted engine."

"And he and your gran—the captain—are good friends," Anne said.

"Yes. Maybe they'll buy that cattle ranch together."

Conversation lagged. Anne could feel Dave studying her face. She watched the moon attempt to peek through the increasing cloud cover, heard the tiny waves lap against the hull as the boat gently swayed on her anchor. Most of all, she tried not to feel anything toward Dave. Maybe he was her cousin. If so, at least she'd know him for the rest of her life. She didn't for one minute think that was a decent substitution for the relationship that was straining to leap into life, but maybe they'd have to settle. One thing was clear: Now that Dave was in the equation, this was no longer a situation she could walk away from.

Dave was almost reclined in the folded sail. He touched Anne's arm and pulled her down until her head rested against his chest. "What's wrong, honey?" he asked gently. His heart thumped soundly beneath her cheek. He ran his hand up her arm, cupping her head, turning it so that her lips were close to his—

"I have to talk to Samuel Bloom," she mumbled.

"What?"

She sat up. "Nothing. It's getting chilly and I'm tired."

He stood and pulled her to her feet, keeping his hand clasped over hers so that she had to pause before leaving.

"Don't be afraid of me," he said softly.

She laughed. "Don't be silly." She felt his gaze on her back as she walked aft toward her own cabin.

Eggs Benedict. What in the world were eggs Benedict? Anne went on deck and found Quincy.

He'd been right—it had begun to rain during the night, and the early-morning sky was gray. The wind was crisp and brisk. Dave and Skip were up forward, fooling with the sails as Quince talked with the captain.

"You want something?" Samuel Bloom asked Anne as she stood by Quince's elbow.

"Ah, no, sir," she mumbled.

" 'Course you do. Wouldn't be lurking around back there if you didn't, would you?"

"Leave the kid alone, Sam," Quince said. He winked at Anne and added, "Is there something you want?"

"Yes. I need to ask you a question. When you have time."

"Sure. You need anything else?" Quince asked the captain.

The captain scowled. "No," he said, resigned to Anne's interference. He turned on his heels and walked forward.

Anne paused for just a second, screwed up her nerve, and said, "Captain? May I talk to you? Not now, but maybe later, when you have the time. That is, if it's not an imposition—"

"Stop equivocating. See me after cabin duty tonight. Quince? We're running late—let's get this boat under way.

Now!'' He marched toward Dave and Skip, barking more orders.

"Don't let him upset you, Missy," Quince said gently. "Sam is a good, decent man. But he doesn't know how to relate to folks real well."

"He does fine with the guests," Anne said, hating the quiver she could hear in her voice.

"Well, that's different. They're guests. You're part of the family now!"

Startled, she jumped. Quince, who was busy stuffing his pipe, was totally unaware how his comment had struck her.

"Now, what is it you wanted?"

"I'm embarrassed to ask you now. It's not important." He waited patiently and she added, "I was just wondering if you had any idea what eggs Benedict are?"

"On Billy's menu? Must be those eggs he makes. Seems to me he puts a fried egg on an English muffin. There may be some ham in there too. Then he tops it with a sauce of some kind. That help?"

Anne grimaced. He ruffled her hair and took off toward the engine. She went below to figure out what the sauce was, proud that she'd made the decision to talk to Samuel Bloom, but nervous about it as well.

Anne had vague memories of her mother creating sauces atop the stove. Unfortunately, those memories did not include recipes. She rummaged through the cupboard and could have wept with relief when she found that the sauce also came in a can. She spared a moment to bless Billy's inebriated soul. The guests ate her version of eggs Benedict like good sports. Even Patty seemed to enjoy the meal, and Anne wondered if the seasick patches were working or if her sudden wellness was due to the fact that the boat was anchored.

The crew had all breakfasted earlier on hot cereal and

toast so they could work on getting *Serenity* ready for the long day's voyage ahead, and the guests were eager to get on deck and watch the anchor come up.

Anne was washing dishes when she heard the engine start and the sound of the electric anchor windlass as it towed the hook up from the bottom of the bay. She wedged herself into a familiar corner so that she wouldn't fall as *Serenity's* hull lifted to her first ocean swell. A sudden wave of nausea reminded her to take her medicine and to remind Patty to put on one of her patches.

She went up on deck an hour later. San Simeon was far behind them now, lost in the swirling mists. The ocean was a deep-gray color, and the waves were capped in white. Quince was talking to the Fontaines.

"It's awfully windy," Lily said. The shorter hair in the front had escaped her braided crown and was troubling her face. She pushed it away. "Won't we tip over?"

"Now don't you worry about that," Quince consoled with a kind chuckle. "Captain got the weather forecast on the radio earlier. It's going to clear off after this little front passes. We're going to have twenty-knot northwesterly winds today—a great sail."

"How fast does the boat go under sail?" John asked.

"Hull speed is twelve knots. We'll make eight or ten today. Cheer up, folks. In an hour this fog will burn off and you'll need your sunscreen. Maybe you'll even see a whale or two. And tonight, after dinner, we'll anchor in a little cove on San Miguel Island."

Anne looked forward. Dave and Skip were raising the sails. The wind caught the fabric and filled it immediately. The engines were turned off, and the *Serenity* came home to her element, happier with her sails filled than bouncing against the waves with the engine. Captain Bloom held the wheel, and Anne spared him a quick glance. It came as no surprise that his expression didn't change when he saw her.

She sat down in the cockpit, hoping the Dramamine would have a chance to work before she had to start thinking of fixing lunch. Boris passed by, and she called out to him.

"How's Patty?"

"Sick again," he said. "I guess the patches don't work."

"Can I get her something to make her feel better? Coffee or tea, anything?"

"She lost that nice breakfast you fixed," he said. He sat next to Anne. His dark toupée was stuffed inside a red knit cap. A huge diamond sparkled in a pinky ring.

"Miserable weather," he said gruffly.

"It'll clear soon," Anne told him, parroting Quince.

"Think so?" He pulled his green coat across his chest and put his feet up against the opposite seat to brace himself. "I spent my life manipulating stocks and bonds. Guess I'm not much of an outdoorsman. Hope the old girl tied herself into that bed," he added.

It took Anne a second to realize the last statement referred to his wife. "Would you like me to go check on Patty for you?" she asked.

"Nice of you to offer."

Anne patted his hand and stood. The boat seemed to be racing away from the fog, the wind at her back. Dave was on the foredeck, his arm around Irene as Liz snapped their photograph. Envy bit at Anne's heart but blew away when Dave looked at her, his handsome face decorated with a grin, his hand raised in a wave.

What right did she have to feel jealous? Irene was turning out to be a nice person. If Dave was her cousin, she should wish a beautiful, wealthy woman would become interested in him. He deserved a woman like Irene. She was happy for him.

"Sure I am," she muttered as she carefully made her way down the companionway ladder to check on Patty.

"I'm going to die," Patty groaned.

Anne tucked the heavy blanket firmly about the older woman's prone body. "No, no. You'll be okay."

"No," Patty protested. "I'm going to die or at least wish I were dead."

"Did you put on a fresh patch?"

Patty pushed back her improbable red hair, and Anne saw a flesh-colored patch on the back of Patty's wrinkled neck.

"Have you tried the pills?" Anne asked. "I . . . hear . . . they work very well."

"Not for me. Oh, I feel sick."

"How about dressing warmly and going up on deck? I know the fresh air will make you feel better. I'll help you."

"Do you really think it will help?" Patty squeaked.

Since to Anne almost anything was better than lying in a bunk down inside, she said with some conviction, "I'm positive."

Patty unstrapped herself and sat on the edge of the bed. She did look awful. As Anne found warm pants and a jacket, Patty told her how this whole trip was Boris's idea.

"I told him I'd get sick, but he told me it was all in my head," she said as Anne coaxed her to put on an extra pair of warm socks. "I told him we should just fly to Rio like we do every winter, but he said he was tired of doing that. He can be so muleheaded. Thank you, dear. Would you look for my red sweater, please? Look in that bottom drawer."

Anne opened the bottom drawer. This cabin was twice as big as hers, all done in teak and sky-blue paint. It was beautiful.

"He told me I could just stay home, but I said no way to that. You must have noticed how attractive younger women find Boris. I tell you, I have to keep my eye on him all the time.''

To her credit, Anne didn't laugh. ''Now for a hat,'' she said, effectively sidestepping the issue of Boris's sex appeal.

''On that hook inside the bathroom door, dear. Thanks. You've been an angel.''

Anne smiled and took Patty's arm. The wind greeted them at the top of the ladder. Boris was still sitting in the cockpit. Liz was sitting next to him—Anne suspected it was because Skip was behind the wheel—and Patty turned to give Anne a look that clearly said, *See there! I told you young women throw themselves at his feet when I'm not around!*

The captain came into the cockpit and asked Patty how she felt. He took her arm from Anne and saw that she was properly ensconced in a portion of the large cockpit-deck area that was a little sheltered from the wind, with one of the wool blankets from under the seat locker firmly tucked around her legs. Then he sat down next to her. Anne turned to find Dave behind her.

''Hello, beautiful,'' he said. The sun was beginning to break through the clouds, and it spilled onto Dave's dark hair and danced in his eyes. Those eyes were the same gray color as the sea and held the same vibrant life and hint of untapped depths. She couldn't help the way her heart smiled when she looked at him, couldn't help the elation being near him made her feel. But fostering these feelings was only going to lead to two broken hearts.

''Morning,'' she said. She took a deep breath and added, ''Where's Irene?''

''Up on the bow with the Fontaines,'' he said.

''She seems very nice,'' she said, pulling up the zipper tab on her jacket. The wind was blowing harder than it had been an hour before and exploited any gap in a person's clothing.

"She is very nice."

"And she certainly seems to like you," she added.

"I'm a likable fellow," he said with a playful grin.

"You two make a nice-looking couple," she said, twisting the knife in her own gut.

He stared at her a moment, his eyes suddenly narrowed and hard. Finally he said, "Anne, if you don't want me to bother you, just say so. Please, don't feel responsible for setting me up with another pretty face. I can take care of myself."

He didn't give her a chance to respond. He turned on his heels and stalked away. Anne felt tears spring into her eyes. She looked toward the horizon and let the cold wind snatch them away. Then she went back below. The menu ordered fresh cookies, and the galley was a safe place to hide.

"Plan a light lunch and an early snack," the captain said a little later that morning. "We'll be rounding Point Arguello late this afternoon, and with this wind and this sea, I expect things to be rough. We'll delay until we're in the Santa Barbara Channel."

"Yes, sir," Anne said. She was down below, helping Skip tidy up the guest cabins. It was one of the few times the captain had spoken to her in a normal voice without a surly undertone, and on the heels of the scene with Dave, she felt weak with gratitude for it. The thought of facing Samuel Bloom that evening, prying into his son's past, perhaps declaring herself his long-lost granddaughter, didn't seem quite so terrifying. He nodded and left. When Anne turned back to her chore, she found Skip staring at her.

"What's the matter?" she asked him as she took off a soiled sheet and stretched a clean one across the foam-rubber mattress.

"You. Do you realize you freeze every time that man comes near? What's the problem?"

Anne tossed a blanket over the sheets. "There is no problem," she said firmly. *Serenity* fell off the side of a rolling wave, and she stumbled against the bunk. "You don't have to change these things every day, do you?"

"Every other. These people aren't used to sleeping on dirty sheets. Did I smell cookies baking earlier?"

Anne nodded as she tucked in the navy-blue bedspread. "Billy said to bake cookies, so I baked cookies. I'm not sure what I'm supposed to do with them."

"Just have them available for people to eat," Skip said. He laughed and added, "Billy always told me that the best way to keep everyone happy was to keep them full and pour the drinks."

"I guess he took his advice to heart," Anne said. "The drinking part, anyway. You know, just between you and me, I can't imagine why the captain fired Billy. I mean, I gather his drinking problem was no secret, and by the organization of the food and supplies in the kitchen, he wasn't a sluggard. Why did the captain decide to fire him the day before a big trip like this one?"

Skip tore the sheet from the second bed and took a new one from Anne. She had already decided this was Irene's and Liz's room because of the two bunks and the accumulation of expensive clothing she'd had to move to make up the first bed. Irene must have brought her entire closet!

"Promise you won't tell?" he said.

Both of them were standing with their legs bent, unconsciously adjusting to the motion of the boat. Anne nodded. "I promise."

"The captain found Billy in his cabin. Not Billy's cabin, mind you. The captain's cabin. He was drunker than a skunk."

Anne smiled. "So he got drunk and went to the wrong cabin. The man could obviously cook and—"

"He wasn't alone, Anne," Skip interrupted. "He was having a private party with the daughter of the couple that had hired the boat for a trip north to San Francisco the week before."

Anne felt her mouth open. "Oh."

"So the captain had to fire him. He said Billy showed 'abysmal judgment.'"

"That sounds like Samuel Bloom," she said.

"He's a very moral man," Skip added, and instantly Anne thought of the letter written to her mother and signed with a capital R. *You know my father—you know what he's like.*

"I'd better check the menu and start lunch," she said, her mouth suddenly dry.

Skip tossed the top sheet across the narrow bunk. "I can finish here. Thanks again for helping out."

"No problem." Anne ducked outside the cabin before Skip noticed she was short of breath. *You know my father— you know what he's like.* Dignified, ultramoral, unforgiving of the love that blossomed too soon between his son and her mother? Was that what he was like? And if it was, would he give her the time of day? *Oh, Mother,* Anne cried silently. *Whether or not I wanted to listen, why didn't you tell me more?*

Billy had obviously understood the *Serenity's* schedule. The menu called for assorted cold cuts and cheese. Anne made a big platter of the meat. She found two kinds of cheese and sliced them thin, then added bottles of different mustards, pickles, and a sliced loaf of rye bread. When she took the first platter into the main salon, she found Dave unlatching the gimbal on the table. It instantly became level, but the boat was so far heeled over, it looked crooked, as it would in a house of mirrors.

He wordlessly took the tray from her hands and set it on the table where it stayed put. He followed Anne back to the galley and took cold imported beer from the refrigerator. Anne placed a bowl of her private recipe cole slaw—grate cabbage, add mayonnaise—on the table along with the freshly baked cookies and stood back to survey the feast, pretending she wasn't aware that Dave stood beside her. Their eyes met, and they both looked down. She ached to tell him she was sorry, but she was afraid that if she did, he'd hug her, and she didn't trust herself to withstand the lure of those arms. So she said nothing.

"I'll tell everyone lunch is ready," he said.

"I'll fix a plate for Patty and Quince," she replied. "Quince is on duty?"

"Quince is on duty."

"Okay."

He went up the ladder, and Anne took two paper plates from the stack. They'd just completed their first postfight conversation, and she hated it.

She ate on deck with Patty and Quince. It was after noon, and she was startled with the change in the weather. Oh, the wind was still blowing, but the sun had burned away the cloud cover, and the ocean was a cobalt-blue color. *Serenity* raced ahead of the wind, her graceful bow lifting to new white-capped swells, then surfing down to the shallow troughs.

"About perfect sailing weather," Quince said between mouthfuls.

Patty, who was just picking at her food, looked at Quince as though he were crazy.

"I thought you preferred the engine to the sails," Anne said.

"When there ain't a drop of wind, I do," he answered. "When the wind is howling on our tail, then I like this." He handed Anne his paper plate and thanked her for lunch. He was attempting to light his pipe one-handed, and Anne took pity on him. She put her own empty plate under his and handed them both to Patty.

"Hold these a second, will you? Here, Quince. Let me take the wheel while you light that thing."

She moved behind the wheel beside him, and he stared at her, his bushy eyebrows half concealing his eyes. "May not be as easy as it looks," he told her. "Okay. Let's see what raw material we've got here."

He moved aside, and Anne took the big wheel. She'd steered Ben Moore's boat many times, but that had been with a long tiller, not a wheel, and it had never been in the open ocean. For a second she was frightened by the power she could feel vibrating through the wood, but she applied some muscle, and *Serenity* sheared off only a little before Anne was in control.

"Keep her headed 158 degrees," Quince said as he lit a match, which the wind promptly extinguished. He turned his back to the wind and lit the match inside his cupped hand. In a minute a puff of smoke announced success.

"How you doing, Missy?" Quince asked as he bit on the pipe stem.

"Fine."

He nodded. "We got some scallops in the foresail. Suppose you can keep her on course while I go fix it?"

"Yes," Anne said. She was busy watching the compass. It was hard to keep the line on 158 degrees, but she was determined to do it. And the life that throbbed in that wheel! She turned it a little both ways. The helm responded ever so slightly, but the mizzen sail flapped unhappily, warning her to get back on course, admonishing her to mind her own business and just let *Serenity* do her own thing.

Anne smiled with the thrill of it. The wind and the hiss of the ocean; the sun and the salty spray; the hum of the canvas as it held the wind—she felt emotion swelling in her chest, filling her with gratitude that no matter what, she was here and experiencing this rush of pleasure.

And then Dave came on deck, and his gaze met hers. He looked startled to see her behind the wheel, and then he looked sad. He turned away and walked forward on the tilting deck to help Quince tighten the foresail. Anne felt her elation deflate, her heart grow heavy. Well, tonight she'd talk to the captain, and tomorrow she'd either tell Dave they were cousins, or she'd throw her arms around his neck and kiss him. If he'd still talk to her. . . .

Chapter Seven

Anne was busy cramming the contents of a package of stuffing mix into a bevy of mushroom caps. She was sick to death of food—of the smell, the sight, the taste, and especially the preparing. The seas had come up, and she was fighting off nausea as she'd forgotten to take a new Dramamine pill after lunch. She swallowed one, muttered, "Come on, baby, kick in," and wondered about Patty Hygrade. The poor woman hadn't eaten a bite of her lunch, and she was apparently afraid to come down inside even though the seas continued to be big and the wind chilly.

The mushroom caps were part of the snack she was supposed to serve before Point Arguello, which was reportedly right ahead. She'd looked at the map after lunch and saw that Point Arguello and Point Conception weren't more than an hour and half apart. She knew the captain was concerned about the weather—he said that with the wind and the currents, the ocean was sure to be rough between the two points. How could anyone possibly be hungry?

But they were. Quince helped her take trays of snacks up on the deck, and while the crew shortened the sails and the sun made its way toward the horizon, they ate the mushrooms and drank white wine.

Anne was pouring Boris another glass of wine and listening to Lily tell Irene about the three whales she and John had spotted at a distance that afternoon, when she heard Dave call her name. She saw that he was in the stern talking to the captain and to Quince. She walked past Skip and Liz, who was watching Skip steer the boat, and joined them.

"I want you to get a movie set up for the guests," Captain Bloom said. "I don't want them up here once the sun goes down."

"What about Patty?" Anne asked, keeping her eyes away from Dave.

"What about her? Oh, you mean her seasickness. Well, help her get in bed if she wants. Has she eaten anything?"

Anne shook her head. "No."

"We'll be anchored off San Miguel Island in five hours," Dave said, his gaze never straying to Anne's face. "Anne can make sure she gets a midnight snack then."

"Good. Okay. We'll get everyone down below and involved in a movie on that confounded machine. Quince, you take the helm while Dave and I get some of the sail down. We'll send Skip down with Anne to help her. I'm going to go below and check the charts again."

They split up. If she hadn't felt miserable about Dave, she would have been excited to be included in the impromptu meeting. As it was, she heard the captain tell everyone that as it was getting dark and cold—he didn't mention rough— would they all go below where Anne would see to it that they had something to do while *Serenity* went around Point Arguello and Point Conception.

Everyone meekly went down below except Patty, who protested. "I'll die down there," she said.

"I'll put you to bed," Anne told her. "And tonight, when we're at anchor, I'll fix you a big dinner."

Patty smiled. "Okay, dear. You just keep an eye on Boris for me, will you?"

Anne smiled and helped Patty down the ladder. She wondered what fun the poor woman could possibly be having and thought that if she were Patty, she'd get off this boat as soon as possible, Boris or no Boris.

It was almost dark. Anne was in the galley cleaning shrimp she'd defrosted earlier in the day. Billy, in some demonic scheme that proved he was impervious to the motion aboard a sailboat, had decreed dinner that night was to be scampi. Anne had never actually eaten scampi, seeing as it was seafood, but she had seen it and heard her father— her stepfather—talk about it. From what she gathered, it was mainly shrimp, garlic, parsley, and lemon juice. She'd just sauté everything in butter and hope for the best.

The movie was almost over, and except for the sound of an actress crying, the boat was quiet. Well, it was quiet if one didn't count all the creaking, groaning, and rattling caused by the ocean and wind. Anne hadn't seen the crew in a while. She was thinking of Dave and her upcoming meeting with his grandfather, when *Serenity* suddenly shuddered. A terrible crash vibrated on the deck above.

One minute Anne was cleaning shrimp, the next, she was on the floor, three pounds of shellfish on top of her, her ankle twisted beneath her, her forehead throbbing from a brief but painful contact with the stove rail. *Serenity* jerked sideways and rolled back, creating an angular, jarring sensation that raced from the top of the mast to the bottom of the keel.

Anne heard frightened screams coming from the main salon. She pushed herself up, ignored the stabbing pain in her ankle, and stumbled toward the noise, scattering shrimp as she moved.

"What was that?" Irene cried. "Did we hit something?"

Anne looked from Liz's wide eyes to Boris's face half ob-
scured by his toupée, which had slid down over his eyes. The
Fontaines held onto each other. Only Irene was on her feet.

"Check on your wife," Anne told Boris. "Make sure
she's okay. Irene, find out if anyone here is hurt. I've got
to go on deck."

She turned away from their frightened faces and climbed
the ladder. There had been no further shudders after the
initial one, but she could hear frantic yelling coming from
outside.

Except for the distant light from the Point Arguello light-
house, it was dark outside. The cold wind whistled past
Anne's ears and stung her face. The ocean was lighter than
the sky and looked enormous.

"Turn on a deck light!" Captain Bloom bellowed.

Anne ducked inside and found the right switch. She went
back outside.

Now the scene was lit, but it didn't make any sense.
Quince was down on his back in the cockpit well, his face
a white mask, his teeth clenched in a painful grimace. He
looked wet. He was clutching his left leg, which twisted at
a weird angle off to the side. Dave had control of the boat
and was hauling in a flapping line connected to the back of
the mizzen boom. Skip wasn't in sight, but Captain Bloom
was kneeling beside Quince. He touched the lower part of
his friend's leg. His hand came away covered in blood.

The howling wind swallowed Anne's cry.

"Rogue wave, Sam," Quince gasped. "A rogue wave.
I never even saw it coming."

"Quiet now," the captain ordered. "Dave, you got
everything under control?"

"She's okay now," Dave said.

"Mizzen sail went into irons," Quince mumbled. "We
broached."

"Yes, yes. I think you've got a compound fracture," the captain said.

Quince groaned. Anne thought she saw his head relax a little and wondered if he was going into shock.

"We've got to get his leg splinted and get him to a hospital," Dave said.

Anne heard a noise behind her and turned to see Skip making his way along the deck slowly, stopping often to hook and unhook his harness tether to the lifeline that ran amidships. The decks looked slippery from seawater. Skip was gasping by the time he got to the cockpit. "I was in the forepeak," he said between breaths. "What happened? Is Quince okay?"

"No," the captain snapped. "You get down below and see what our passengers need. Anne, you come up here and stay with Quince. Dave, I'll take the wheel if you'll look into our emergency medical supplies. We'll get him stabilized; then we'll call the Coast Guard."

Dave and his grandfather exchanged places. Dave squeezed Anne's arm as he walked past her.

"You go put on a harness," he said.

"But I have to help Quince—"

"That rogue wave washed right into the boat, Anne. If Quince hadn't been wearing his harness, he'd have probably been washed overboard. Do as I say."

She did as he said. She then knelt beside Quince and cradled his head in her lap. She could feel his body trembling through his wet clothes. The lower half of the left leg of his jeans was dark with blood. His face was pale in the overhead light, almost the same color as his hair. Anne opened the nearest locker and felt the coarse texture of the wool blanket. She dragged it from the locker and draped it over Quince, noticing for the first time that she was cold too.

"Shouldn't we get him into something warm?" Anne asked.

The captain yanked on a line and turned the wheel to his left. "I'm afraid to move him till we get his leg immobilized," he said. "Between these two points of land, the ocean can be a bear." He dug around in his pocket, emerging at last with a pocket knife, which he handed to Anne. "Cut the leg off those pants. Hold on now, a big wave is sneaking up on us."

Anne braced her elbows and knees against the cockpit well and tried to keep Quince still. *Serenity* lifted and fell. The gray giant swept off toward the coast.

She pulled the blanket off his left leg and carefully started sawing on the sea-drenched denim above Quince's knee, timing her cuts between waves. It was slow going. Before she got far, Dave erupted into the cockpit. His face was pale with concern. He made a place for himself on the other side of Quince and opened the emergency medical kit.

"Let me," he said, taking the knife from Anne. With a few deft strokes he hacked away the jeans. Quince's eyes were closed, but he opened them as the cold steel of the knife touched his skin.

"Don't go cutting off my leg, boy," he said through gritted teeth.

Dave grinned at him.

"Is anyone else hurt?" Samuel Bloom asked his grandson.

"No. They're a little shaken up and worried about Quince. I don't think he'd be hurt if the mizzen boom hadn't yanked around and knocked him down. He must have broken his leg against the cockpit seat when he fell."

"I hit the finders bar on the binnacle," Quince mumbled, pointing a shaking finger toward the beautiful brass compass stand.

"Hang on, you tough old goat," the captain said. "Here's another big one—hold on."

Anne and Dave braced Quince between them. Dave pulled the denim away, and Anne gasped.

"Get ahold of yourself, girl!" the captain growled. "If you can't, go below and send Skip out here." The wave passed beneath them with a sinister hiss.

"Leave the girl alone," Quince muttered.

Anne fought back tears of embarrassment and stroked Quince's forehead. She hadn't meant to gasp, but the shagged end of his shinbone was poking through his skin, and blood was dripping down his white skin through the gash in his leg. She took a deep breath.

Dave said, "Hand me the splint."

She saw that along with the medical kit, he'd hauled a ready-made plastic splint into the cockpit. She handed it to Dave, who set it beside Quince's left leg.

"Support his back and shoulders while I lift his leg," Dave demanded, sounding, for the first time, like his grandfather. Anne did as told. Dave guided the mangled leg into the wraparound splint and Velcroed it closed.

Quince's eyes flew open, and he swore loudly. For some reason the swear reassured Anne, and she smiled at him.

"Sorry, Quince," Dave said. He sat back on his heels. "Not much else we can do for now." He looked at Anne. She was startled to see a hint of amusement steal into his eyes. "Do you know you smell like shrimp?" he said at last.

"She's got one tangled up in her hair," Quince mumbled.

Dave reached across Quince and pulled and yanked, producing at last one tired-looking shrimp wrapped in several of Anne's hairs. He tossed it overboard. His eyes narrowed, and he said, "What happened to your forehead?"

Anne was suddenly aware of a dull ache above her right eyebrow. She felt a lump. "It's not important," she told him.

"The girl's right," Samuel Bloom interrupted. "Take this wheel so I can call the Coast Guard. We've got to get Quince off this boat and into a hospital."

"We'll look at that later," Dave told Anne. He extracted himself from the cockpit and took the wheel. Samuel Bloom opened the aft hatch that led down to his cabin and disappeared. A moment later Anne heard his voice and the cackling answer of the Coast Guard. She gripped Quince's hand and squeezed it.

The sails came down, and the engine came on. It took an hour and a half to get around the sea horn off Point Conception. The mournful wailing echoed Anne's nerves. Skip had brought out another blanket, and they'd wrapped it around Quince. Dave had told Skip to find a coat for Anne, and he'd delivered this and helped her shrug it on over the harness and in the confines of the cockpit well. They decided to leave Quince alone. With two wool blankets around him, his teeth had stopped chattering. In fact, he'd grown very quiet, and Anne was scared he was in shock. His lips looked white in the artificial lights beaming down from the spreaders. She was almost glad when Dave turned them off so that he could regain some vestige of night vision.

Anne gathered from eavesdropping on various conversations that there was a small cove called Coho around Point Conception and that the *Serenity* was making for it. The Coast Guard was sending a helicopter from their air station in Los Angeles that was to meet them there. Anne also heard Quince say he wasn't being airlifted into some "whirlybird" like a load of cod, and the captain's answering challenge, "You want to make a bet on that?"

It took an hour and twenty-two minutes—the longest hour and twenty-two minutes Anne had ever lived through—to reach Coho. During that time the captain had sporadic conversations with the Coast Guard. Anne heard him answer many questions as the proper forms were filled out even as help was racing toward them.

Coho was dark and desolate. They set the anchor and switched the deck lights back on. Within five minutes they all heard the welcome beat of a helicopter approaching from the south.

The customers were all sitting on the cabin or standing on the decks. Even Patty had gotten up. The wind had died down, and the water was relatively calm within the cove. The copter turned on its searchlight, and suddenly the small cove was illuminated in fits and starts.

"Should be a pretty stable platform for the rescue," Dave told his grandfather as they both looked toward the approaching helicopter. "You ever do anything like this before?"

"Once," Samuel Bloom said. "In Florida. Lady had appendicitis."

"Bet they're back on the radio," Dave said.

The captain nodded briskly and ducked inside his private hatch. He reappeared a second later, the handpiece of the VHF held against his mouth.

"We see you, Coast Guard, over," he said.

Anne heard the seaman's voice, the background noise from the helicopter loud through the speaker. He told them to secure Quince in a life jacket for the ride to the helicopter.

Dave rustled around in a locker. Anne helped Quince sit and tried to ignore the gasps of pains that escaped, unbidden and unappreciated, from his mouth. Dave gently put the old man's hands through the armholes and buckled the vest securely around his chest. Meanwhile the seaman was filling them in on how to secure Quince into the litter once it was dropped, checking first to make sure they'd splinted the leg.

The helicopter was above and slightly to the left of the *Serenity* by now, hovering there like a spaceship, almost invisible to the passengers aboard *Serenity* because of the glare from the searchlight pointing down and flooding *Serenity* with white light. The water around the boat was beaten flat, its surface heavily rippled and gray. *Serenity* practically stopped bobbing in the small waves, stabilizing in the tremendous downdraft. Conversely, the blankets and ropes all sprang to life. Everyone grabbed something to keep it from flying away.

The Stokes litter, as Anne heard it called, descended toward them. It was about six feet long, with eight-foot pontoons secured to either side. Anne decided the only reason it would need pontoons would be so that it would float if they lost it. Quince apparently decided the same thing.

"Those kids better not drop me," he mumbled, but only Anne was close enough to hear over the roar of the helicopter.

"Looks like that thing is roosting on our main mast," Dave yelled. He caught the end of the litter. John Fontaine appeared at his side, and together with the captain they guided the litter across the lifeline and onto the port cockpit seat.

Fighting the wind created by the helicopter rotor blades, John and Dave helped Quince stand on his right leg. Anne supported his left leg. On the count of three, the two younger men lifted Quince beneath his arms while Samuel Bloom helped Anne with his legs, and they deposited him gently into the basketlike litter. Dave and Anne fastened the belts across his body and bulky clothes.

Quince grimaced. Anne leaned down and kissed his prickly cheek.

"Where's my pipe?" he asked.

Dave leaned down. "What?"

"He wants his pipe," Anne shouted.

Dave tucked the edge of a blanket around Quince's shoulder. "Time to quit smoking," he said.

Captain Bloom was back on the radio, his voice raised to be heard. "He's ready to go, over," he said.

"That's fine, *Serenity*," the Coast Guard answered. "We'll take him to Santa Barbara, over."

"We surely thank you for your help," the captain added.

"Right. Guide the litter off the seats and watch your hands and heads," the Coast Guard answered.

Anne saw the captain pat his friend's shoulder before the litter began to rise. Everyone aboard seemed to holler, "Good luck, Quince," at the same time. Dave and John guided the litter as it slowly rose; then it was above their heads and out of their reach.

"We've got him," the Coast Guard said on the radio. The searchlight went off, and the copter lifted away from the sailboat, whisking Quince off to safety. Within a few hours he'd be in an operating room.

No one spoke. The air was still and quiet after the disturbance of the helicopter, and then suddenly it wasn't as the wind reasserted itself and the water began slapping the hull once again. The captain coughed, and suddenly the passengers were full of talk.

Anne saw something dark on the cockpit floor and bent down to retrieve Quince's pipe. She clutched it in her hand and met Dave's steady gaze. "Wish you could fly away too?" he asked.

Anne sagged against him and didn't answer.

Chapter Eight

"We'll stay here for the night," Captain Bloom said, his voice haggard. "It's still blowing out there, and besides, everyone is too worn-out to make for San Miguel Island tonight. Okay, boys, let's get this boat into shape for the night. Skip, you and Dave check the anchor line. Anne, you'd better get working on dinner."

"I think she's hurt," Dave said.

Captain Bloom glared at Anne, daring her to wimp out on them when she was needed. She wouldn't have dreamed of giving him the satisfaction. "I'm fine," she insisted, standing straight again.

"No, you're not—"

"Young man, when the girl makes sense, listen to her. You can see to that bump later when there's time."

Anne ignored the throbbing in her ankle and head. "That's right," she agreed.

Dave shook his head and went forward with Skip. Anne went below. If memory served her, there were about sixty shrimp and a few chopped green onions on the galley floor. And no matter how traumatic the last two hours had been, no matter how rattled people were or how worried about Quince, she had no doubts they would be hungry.

94

"Miss Moore," Boris said as she stepped off the ladder. His toupée was back in place, and he'd tied one of the galley aprons around his waist. There was a glint in his watery eyes that Anne had never detected before. There was also an unfamiliar aroma in the air.

"Please sit down," he said, pointing at the long seat opposite the table. The Fontaines were sitting there already. John patted the place next to him.

Anne sat. John handed her a glass. Boris produced a bottle of brandy and half filled her glass. "What's going on?" Anne asked. "And what is that delicious smell?"

"Chicken Marengo," Irene said from the galley. "Patty and I are cooking."

"They needed white wine for the sauce," Boris explained, holding up another bottle. "We ran into the brandy while we were liberating one from the cache in the engine room."

Patty appeared behind Irene's shoulder. "Hope it was okay to use the chicken breasts I found in the freezer, dear."

"Yes," Anne mumbled, close to tears, their kindness overwhelming her. Patty must have come back to life when they anchored the boat and the motion all but stopped.

"That's quite a knot on your forehead," John said. He pushed aside Anne's hair and peered at it. "The skin isn't broken."

"But you are limping," Lily noted. "I saw you favor your right foot when you walked over here."

"I twisted my ankle when I fell," Anne said. For the first time she noticed brandy glasses in every hand and roses in every cheek. Actually, it wasn't a bad idea—she was surprised the captain hadn't thought of it.

"I washed the shrimp real good, and we cooked it," Irene told her.

"Oh, you didn't have to do that," Anne said, standing abruptly. Her head twirled around, and her ankle protested.

Boris gently pushed her back onto the seat. "Sit still. Patty makes a mean cocktail sauce."

"Which reminds me," Patty sang from the galley. "Do we have any horseradish?"

Anne felt her lower lip tremble; then much to her chagrin she burst into tears and John Fontaine folded her in comforting arms.

An hour later there was a knock on her cabin door. Anne had just gotten out of the shower. She pulled on gray sweatpants and a large blue sweatshirt, then called, "Come in."

The door opened and Dave entered, closing the door softly behind him. While the door was open, Anne could hear the guests laughing as they drank the captain's brandy and cooked dinner for the crew. There was a kind of benign mutiny going on that extended outside as well as inside. Before Anne had taken her shower, she'd seen Liz and John climb the ladder and heard them tell the others they were going to "help put this boat to bed."

"Who's in charge out there?" Anne asked.

Dave smiled as he looked around the cabin, his eyes lingering on a photo of Quince and the captain. "Patty and Boris Hygrade. They've got the captain sandwiched on the inside of the table between Skip and Irene, and they're force-feeding him his best port. I'd say the customers are definitely in control."

His breath smelled faintly of brandy—obviously he'd been urged to fortify himself too. Anne laughed softly and hoped the captain was taking the whole thing in good humor. With her luck, he'd think she'd engineered the take-over to relieve herself of her duties, and he'd have her strapped to the main mast and whipped with soggy seaweed.

"I don't know what happened to them," Anne said as she sat on the edge of the bunk. "One minute they're mindless sheep, and the next thing we know, they're raiding the refrigerator and the wine cellar—as it were—and making meals. That chicken smells delicious."

Dave sat on the bunk beside her. "Patty said to tell you dinner will be ready in a few minutes. And Lily told me your ankle is hurt."

"It's nothing," she said softly, unconsciously touching her foot.

He moved her hand aside and tenderly probed the area with gentle fingers. "It's a little swollen," he said.

"It's nothing," she repeated.

He moved his hand up her leg, then her arm, gently touched the bump on her forehead, then caressed her cheek.

"I think the bump is just a bump," he said softly. His eyes were deep pools, inviting her to enter. "Anne—"

She caught his hand and held it firmly in hers. His body immediately stiffened. "I keep forgetting. You don't feel the same way about me that I feel about you."

"I'm . . . I'm sorry, Dave." She felt a tear run down her cheek. He looked into her eyes; then he touched the tear with a fingertip. "Your eyes are so blue," he whispered. "They're as blue as the captain's, but deeper and softer."

Anne felt more tears fill her eyes.

"I don't understand," he said. "If you don't love me, Anne, why are you crying? Why—"

A knock interrupted him. "Dinner is ready," Patty chirped. "Come and get it!"

Anne stood up, wincing as she forgot about her ankle and put her weight on it. "Let's go," she said, wiping her sleeve across her face to erase the tears.

"I'm not letting you off the hook that easily," Dave answered as he stood. He looked down at her and added,

"Something is going on, and I intend to find out what it is!"

"Dave—"

"Not now," he said, pushing open the cabin door. Then he was gone. Anne hobbled out after him.

Dinner that night was the best since they'd set sail. No one was unkind enough to say it, but Anne wasn't a fool. She could taste the subtle seasonings a good cook knew to add, and she just hoped her cooking wasn't the reason Patty Hygrade was sick half the time. She also wondered if Samuel Bloom would realize the difference and cable Billy: *Come back!*

The captain was taking the mutiny in good spirits. He actually spared Anne half a smile and a kind question about how she was feeling, but she thought it was probably done more to reassure the passengers that he wasn't an ogre than because of any sudden concern about her minor injuries.

They opened three bottles of wine and toasted Quince; then the captain told them all that he'd like to speak to them.

"We have two options," he said. "Number one, we go to Santa Barbara and let you people go ashore. I'll refund your money, and you can go on home."

"Is the trip unsafe because Quince isn't aboard anymore?" John asked.

"No, no. As important as Quince is around here, I select my crew on the basis of overlap. There isn't any one of us that is one hundred percent necessary to the safety or comfort of this boat and its passengers." He paused and added, "Except for our cook, maybe."

Anne smiled at the intended compliment. The passengers had just disproved that theory, however, and she knew it.

"Does that include you, Captain?" Patty asked, her voice a trifle slurred with brandy and wine.

The captain appeared to consider his answer before he said, "Yes, of course. As for the hole left by Quince's absence, Dave is perfectly capable of keeping the engines running. We'll all pitch in and cover Quince's other chores and his watches."

"I can help with his watches too," Anne offered, remembering the few short moments she'd been in control earlier that day and the feel of the helm as it came alive in her hands.

"Quince said she was a natural," Boris said with a broad wink.

"What's the second option?" Lily asked.

The captain cleared his throat. "We go on as scheduled, with a slight modification due to the time we've lost here. That means we bypass San Miguel Island and head straight for Santa Catalina Island, then on to San Diego, et cetera."

John said, "I propose a third option. Let's go to Santa Barbara so that you people can make sure Quince is okay."

"I can use the radio to ascertain that," the captain said quickly. "You people don't have to sacrifice—"

"We all like Quince," John interrupted. There was a general murmur of agreement, and he continued. "And I assure you that I am not talking sacrifice. My great-aunt lives in Santa Barbara. One call and she'll have a car down at the marina to take us all on a rousing tour of the place."

"I've always wanted to see the missions," Liz said with her customary zeal.

"And there's a wonderful shopping area," Irene said.

"Is everyone in agreement?" John asked.

Anne watched every head nod. The captain looked flustered.

"So, tomorrow morning, Captain Bloom, we'd appreciate it if you were to take us to Santa Barbara where you'll leave our entertainment up to me. Aunt Frances has a huge house on the ocean, plenty of room for everyone. She'll be thrilled to have the chance to throw a small party for my new bride. We'll all spend the night there, report back early the day after tomorrow, and continue south.''

''I—I,'' the captain sputtered.

''Just nod,'' Dave said dryly. ''I wouldn't try to cross them tonight, and you know you're dying to see Quince.''

Everyone laughed as Samuel Bloom gave up and nodded his head.

''Anne?''

She'd fallen asleep on the settee while everyone else talked. She awoke with a start and found Captain Bloom leaning over her. The lights were dimmed; the boat rolled gently on her anchor. The captain straightened up when he saw her eyes flutter open.

She'd been dreaming about him. In the dream he'd confirmed her suspicions about being his granddaughter, and he'd welcomed her with open arms. She'd felt such warmth and safety as he held her; then she'd looked over his shoulder and seen Dave and realized that even if she won, she lost. Either way she lost.

''Anne? Are you okay?''

She sat up. ''Fine,'' she mumbled. ''Where is everyone?''

''Gone to bed.'' He sat down across from her. She could see the soft light reflected in his steely blue eyes. He folded his arms across his chest and said, ''I thought I'd made a mistake.''

''Mistake?''

''Dave wanted me to send you to the hospital with Quince. He was concerned about that lump. But I didn't think it was serious.''

"It's not," she assured him. "I don't know why I'm so tired."

"We're all tired," he said, and for the first time since she'd met him, he looked his age. He rubbed at his eyes and then looked back at her. There was a note of reprimand in his voice as he added, "Dave didn't want anyone to disturb you tonight, but it's not fitting for a member of the crew to sleep in the salon."

How he could go from being a concerned old man to a demanding despot in the space of a heartbeat!

"Besides, you wanted to speak to me about something."

"Yes, I did. I. . . ." She paused and felt her questions freeze in her throat. Maybe he was a despot, but her earlier observation held true—he was dead tired. "It's too late tonight," she said. "It can wait."

He nodded, as though relieved not to have to deal with anything else that evening. The next thing she knew, he was standing and pulling her to her feet. "You'll find our passengers' mutiny in the galley didn't extend to washing up the dishes," he said dryly. "I'll have Skip wake you early so that you can get the galley shipshape before we pull up the anchor and run to Santa Barbara tomorrow morning."

"Okay," she said, her spirits at an all-time low.

He took a step away, then turned around. "I'm glad you're aboard, young lady."

Her spirits shot to the sky, but he detonated them early, before they could burst. "If you weren't here, I'd have to cook now, and I'm even worse at it than you are. Good night, Anne."

"Good night, Captain," she said and wearily made her way through the messy galley to her own bed.

Drilling platforms. Anne didn't think she'd ever seen

anything as ugly as an oil-drilling platform sticking up out of the blue Pacific Ocean, its metal framework an eyesore and potential environmental disaster. Anne clipped a couple of damp dish towels to the lifelines and stole a quick peek at Dave. He was behind the wheel, Irene standing behind him, Liz on his right. Irene's lush blond mane was still damp from her morning shower, and she had both hands on Dave's shoulders. He met Anne's gaze and spared an impersonal smile, as though to nail home the fact that she'd erected barriers and he'd observe them—at least as long as it suited his purpose.

It had taken Anne over two hours to eradicate the mess Patty and Irene had made preparing chicken Marengo, which she supposed proved that she was needed aboard, after all. The lump on her forehead had gone down over the night, but her ankle still ached, and she favored it without even noticing she was doing so.

John Fontaine spent half the morning on the radio arranging the day with his great-aunt. Anne concentrated on chores, trying to keep her mind off Quince, Samuel Bloom, and Dave. Patty donned another motion-sickness patch and sat in the cockpit, looking miserable.

Gulls wheeled overhead as they traveled into Santa Barbara. The boat had barely tied up to the dock when a uniformed chauffeur escorting an elderly woman with bluish-white hair appeared. John greeted his great-aunt and introduced her to the crew and passengers. One by one the guests disembarked with overnight totes, their faces full of excitement, their voices light. All except Irene, who stopped in front of Dave and said, ''Are you sure you won't change your mind, Dave? I know the others would be thrilled to have you along.''

Anne had changed into a white cotton T-shirt and a white skirt, both a little damp and wrinkled from being crammed in a drawer. Irene was wearing beige natural-silk walking shorts and a crisp pink blouse. Anne couldn't help being curious how Irene managed to keep her clothes looking like that aboard a sailboat.

"I want to go to the hospital with the captain to check on Quince," Dave said.

"Afterward, then," she persisted. "John can give you the address—"

"I have something I have to do after the hospital," he said, injecting a hint of regret in his voice.

Apparently the regret satisfied Irene. She nodded and followed the others down the dock toward the waiting black limousine.

"She didn't even look back," Skip said with a laugh as he punched Dave's arm.

"She's not the kind of woman to look back," Dave told him. "Let's get the sails stored away and go see Quince."

Anne crammed into the taxi with the *Serenity's* three remaining male crew members. The men didn't say a word as they rode to the hospital. They all pretended they weren't worried about Quince, but they all were, and they all knew it. Anne thought men were strange creatures indeed, though the male reticence rubbed off on her, too, as she kept her mouth closed and her fears to herself. But Quince was old, and his leg had been horribly mangled. Even if he was okay, would he walk normally, and if he couldn't, would he ever set sail on the *Serenity* again? And if he couldn't sail. . . .

Quince was asleep in a room by himself. His left leg was ensconced in plaster from the knee to the foot and suspended above the bed with ropes and wires. His skin was about the same color as the plaster and looked more fragile than it had the day before. Anne had bought a single blue carnation in the gift shop downstairs, and she put it in his hands as she leaned down to kiss his forehead.

He opened his eyes, looked at Anne, looked at the flower, blinked his eyes, and then saw Samuel Bloom.

"Holy Neptune!" he muttered.

The captain patted his friend's shoulder. "How are you, you old fake?"

Quince blinked a couple of times. When he spoke, his voice was hoarse and thin. "I thought I'd died. Anne looks like an angel, all in white like that." He reached for a container of water on the tray that hovered over his bed. Skip picked up the glass and directed the straw somewhere under Quince's drooping mustache.

"Well, I can see we worried about you for nothing," Dave said. "You look better than the rest of us put together."

"Natural good looks," he muttered, but Anne noticed the way he winced when he turned his body to face Dave.

"I brought you a few of your things," Dave said, lifting a small canvas suitcase.

Skip had picked out a couple of western paperback books at the newsstand while Anne bought the flower. He put them on the tray with the water glass. "I know you like Louis L'Amour."

"I sure do," Quince said. He looked at Samuel Bloom and added, "What did you bring me?"

"Myself and a checkerboard," the captain said, producing a pint-sized board from his pocket.

"Anyone find my pipe?" Quince asked.

Anne produced the pipe she'd found in the cockpit, no worse for wear. "I even brought you a pouch of tobacco," she told him.

"They're not going to let him smoke in here," the captain said sternly.

"This would be a good time for you to quit that foul thing," Dave added.

Quince started to protest, but he heard the approaching footsteps of a nurse and clumsily hid the pipe and pouch in the folds of the blanket.

Miss Ynez, RN, bustled into the room, her starched white uniform in stark contrast with the motherly look of concern lurking in the brown depths of her eyes. "Mr. Adams," she said, pushing past Anne and Skip. "One visitor at a time, you scamp." She plumped his pillow and attempted to adjust the blanket, but Quince fought her off.

She put her hands on her waist and regarded him with narrowed eyes. "You are not a cooperative patient," she scolded.

He returned her look, but Anne saw his elbow firmly planted on the cache hidden under the blanket. "Busybody," he said.

Captain Bloom cleared his throat. "We're sorry, nurse. It's our fault. We're shipmates and we were worried about him."

"He's going to be okay," the nurse informed him. "His doctor comes in about two hours. You can stay and talk to him if you'd like."

"That's fine," the captain said. He turned to Dave and Anne and Skip and added, "The rest of you can leave. I'll stay here awhile and take Quince's mind off his troubles by beating him at checkers."

"You wish," Quince muttered.

Nurse Ynez shook her finger at Quince. "I'll call the doctor if you don't mind me, Mr. Adams," she threatened. When she turned to leave, Anne saw a glimmer of humor in those beautiful eyes, and the two women exchanged bemused smiles.

"Nosy female," Quince said as he pulled his treasures

out from under the blanket. He lovingly examined the pipe, and Anne suspected she hadn't done him any favors.

"You're not going to light that, are you?" she asked.

"Sure I am," he said defiantly; then he lay back against his pillow and chuckled. "Later. After Miss Ynez gets off duty."

The captain pulled a chair over and sat down beside Quince's bed. "You children run along," he said. "Boat leaves port for Catalina at nine o'clock tomorrow morning. Don't be late."

Out on the sidewalk, Skip produced a slip of paper with the name and address of a Mexican restaurant written on it. "Liz invited me to meet everyone for dinner," he said. "Are you two coming?"

"Not me," Anne said.

"You go ahead," Dave told Skip. "Anne and I have an appointment."

Skip caught a passing taxi, and Dave and Anne started walking, Anne doing her best to hide her limp.

"What's this about an appointment?" she asked.

"You owe me a dinner."

"But—"

"No. Remember that afternoon in San Simeon? I asked you out to dinner, and you accepted. In fact, you promised."

"San Simeon seems like a long time ago," she said sadly. San Simeon was the last place she'd felt free to love Dave, the last place they'd kissed. She'd felt a new door opening, and then that night the door had slammed in her face.

"I know it seems like a long time ago. But it was only two days ago, back when you liked me."

"I still like you," she scoffed.

"No, you don't. Now you're afraid of me, and I want to know why."

"Dave—"

"Not now. After a fancy gourmet dinner. After I ply you with champagne and caviar. Oh, that's right, you don't like fish. Okay, after I ply you with champagne and beer nuts. Your ankle still hurts." Right on cue, a taxi passed by and Dave hailed it. "Let's go," he told her, motioning her inside.

Anne made up her mind. If it was the truth he wanted, then it was the truth he'd get. Maybe he knew about his uncle. Maybe he'd heard rumors about a baby or about Serena. Maybe he could provide answers so that she could present herself as a proven fact to Samuel Bloom instead of a question mark. Besides, almost anything was better than letting Dave think she didn't care about him. It was only fair to put his mind and heart to rest and to show him why their love wasn't meant to be.

Chapter Nine

"Well?" Dave asked.

"I still don't know what it is," Anne confided. They were discussing the meal they'd just finished. The moussaka had been served in a bowl nestled inside a colorful wicker basket, and they'd both eaten three helpings.

"Fancy eggplant," Dave said. "I have a little cookbook, so I looked it up and discovered it was a Greek specialty."

"You have a cookbook?" Anne almost screeched. She lowered her voice. "You have a cookbook aboard the *Serenity*!"

Dave's eyebrows shot up his forehead. "Yes. It's just a little one. Why?"

Anne laughed and shook her head. It was too late now, but what she would have given three days before for a cookbook! "It doesn't matter," she said, then looking about at the other diners' plates full of fried chicken and prime ribs added, "This isn't a Greek restaurant."

"It's amazing what an advance phone call and a bribe can accomplish. Did you enjoy it?"

"It was delicious," she said. "The restaurant is so pretty, and the wine was ambrosia. Everything was perfect."

Dave leaned back in his chair and dazzled her with a broad smile. "Good. Do you want dessert?"

"Couldn't eat another bite," she insisted. Now that dinner was over, could question-and-answer time be far behind? She felt her stomach tighten into knots.

"Don't look so scared," he said, accurately assessing her unease. "I'm not going to pounce on you right this minute. Besides, all I want to know is how you can resist my boyish good looks and overwhelming charm. I mean, it's not as though you're being shot in front of a firing squad at dawn."

"No," she agreed.

Dave paid the check and held Anne's hand as they walked out into the February evening. It might be the middle of winter, but the bougainvillea were blooming, and the warm air was heavy with their perfume. Anne took her hand from Dave's as she got into yet another taxi. Within minutes they were back at the marina.

Serenity was docked at the end of a finger large enough to accommodate her. Bathed in moonlight, she was a long, dark form, a floating world of shadows. Dave knew his way around the deck, and he helped Anne climb up the boarding ladder and into the cockpit. His hand lingered on her arm, burning her skin.

After he unlocked the main hatch, he turned and took Anne into his arms. She meant to push away but felt powerless in his embrace. His lips were warm, demanding, intoxicating. She was suddenly inflamed, too, and returned his kiss with longing of her own. Reason nibbled at the corners of her mind. She finally turned her face and tried to wrench away.

"Keep telling yourself you don't feel anything but friendship for me,'' he said huskily, his hands gripping her upper arms.

"Dave—"

"But don't expect me to believe it." He let go of her, pushed back the hatch cover, and folded back the mahogany doors. "I'll go first and light the lamp so you can see."

Anne saw his dark shape disappear down the darker hatch. Her knees were suddenly weak, and she leaned against the cabin top. She could still feel his mouth, his hands. . . . With a sigh, she followed him inside *Serenity*.

He lit the large hanging lamp and replaced the glass mantle. As he turned up the light, the interior of the *Serenity* assumed friendly proportions, and Anne was reminded that to her, this ship was becoming more of a home than any she'd occupied since her parents had died. It wrenched her heart to think of ever leaving it, though she knew that day was going to come, and not that far in the future, either. Even if the captain proved to be her grandfather, the kiss she'd just shared with Dave ruled out any possibility that the two of them could coexist as cousins, at least right away.

"You're a million miles from here," Dave said as he unlocked the liquor cabinet. The ship's clock ticked away the minutes. It seemed to Anne that he avoided looking directly at her the same way she avoided looking directly at him.

"There are so many things to think about," she explained. "I wonder where everyone is."

"The captain must still be with Quince."

"Hmm—" She summoned up an ounce of humor, about all she had left. "I think it's more interesting that Skip is still with Liz."

Dave chuckled as he found a half-full bottle of brandy and poured a healthy dollop into two glasses. He put one glass down in front of Anne and raised his in a silent toast.

"Why don't you ever call the captain Grandpa or Grand-father?" she asked as she swirled the amber liquid in the snifter.

He sat down across from her. "I guess because I was almost twenty-four before I ever met him," he said. "I mean, met him as an adult. It's never seemed natural to either one of us to get mushy."

"Quince said you were trying to prove yourself. What did he mean?"

"Quince said that?" He took a sip of brandy as he thought and added, "I guess he meant that I wanted to prove I was aboard *Serenity* because I deserved to be, not because I was the captain's grandson. Hey, I'm the one who's supposed to be asking the questions."

"Do you remember your uncle?" Anne asked.

"Uncle Ron? Not much. Why do you want to know about him?"

"Just humor me," she said without looking up.

After a long silence Dave said, "My mother has pictures of Ron and Dad together. They looked like flip sides of the same coin. Both had dark hair, but Dad's eyes were blue like the captain's eyes, and Ron's were gray like mine. Mom says I favor Uncle Ron, and even the captain mentioned it the first time he saw me all grown up."

Anne felt her throat close. Was that what she'd felt when she first saw Dave? Had it been recognition of her own flesh and blood and not the intense romantic love she'd taken it for? She looked at him closely, trying to see her father in his gray eyes, and seeing at last only Dave.

"Did you like him?" Anne asked softly.

His smile had a wistful quality. "Yes, of course. He was a lot younger than my father, no more than a kid himself. He laughed a lot and loved to water-ski. Mom said that he was an awful tease and that I was his favorite target. He'd tickle me till I thought I was going to go crazy. I'd beg him to stop, and then Dad would tackle him, and we'd all roll around on the floor, laughing and carrying on.''

Anne saw Dave's eyes fill with tears that he hastily wiped away with his fingers. He paused a second and said, "You know, I don't believe I've ever recalled that before."

"My father died before I was born," she said.

"But I thought you said you and he went sailing—"

"Ben Moore was my stepfather. Oh, he couldn't have loved me any more had I been his own daughter, and I couldn't have loved him any more. But the truth of the matter is that my mother never finished high school. She dropped out to have me, and though I have reason to believe she and my . . . my biological . . . father had plans to marry before I was actually born, they never did."

Dave put his hand over hers. "Are you worried I'll think less of you because your mother wasn't married? Anne, I assure you that kind of thing couldn't mean less to me."

She met his gaze. "I hadn't thought of that," she confided. "No, what I'm worried about is a lot more complicated."

"What then?"

She took a deep breath. It was now or never. "I didn't really come aboard the *Serenity* to apply for the job of cook," she began. "I came to find some part of the family I'd never known. I knew that if I was right, my father was dead, but I had reason to believe my grandfather was alive."

She stopped talking. The words just weren't there. She met Dave's gaze and saw the first signs of realization dawn in his face as his eyes narrowed and his mouth formed a straight line.

"What are you saying?" he demanded.

"Samuel Bloom," she whispered.

Dave stared at her. He opened his mouth and closed it without uttering a word. He took his hand away from hers, and still he stared at her.

Anne evaded his eyes by peering into her brandy snifter. "My father, my biological father, wrote my mother a letter because he'd rejected her when she told him she was pregnant, and he felt awful about it. He promised her he'd make it up to her. My mother kept that letter—I found it after she died. In the letter he told her his father wouldn't understand her condition and begged her to give him till after graduation to confess the whole thing to him. I don't know for sure what happened. All I have is the letter, dated several months before my birth." She looked up at him and blurted it out. "Dave, I think my father might be your Uncle Ron!"

Dave studied her face with eyes that didn't appear to see. "What was your mother's name?" he asked at last.

"Serena Cole."

"Serena?"

"Yes. And my father called her his 'Serenity.'"

"Good Lord." He took a healthy swallow of brandy. "Didn't he sign this letter? Can't you tell if Ron Bloom was your father by his signature?"

"He signed it with a capital R, as though it were common for him to do so. Listen, Dave, I know this is a shock."

"There's an understatement."

"They loved each other," she said defensively.

"Please, don't accuse me of puritanical morality I don't feel," he snapped. "I don't care if Ron Bloom fathered five hundred kids before his untimely death. That way I'd have five hundred cousins. I grew up lonely, Anne, and I'd love to discover an extended family almost as much as you would. But I don't want it to be you." His voice softened as he added, "I had other plans for you."

Anne saw her own misery reflected in his eyes. "When

Quince told me you were the captain's grandson, I felt as though someone had stabbed me in the heart,'' she mumbled.

He sighed heavily. "Well, where do we go from here?"

"We?"

"Seems to me we're in this together," he said. He tossed down the last of his brandy and met her gaze straight on. "I want to know the truth. Why don't we begin with you telling me everything you know?"

She felt tears roll down her cheeks, and he took her in his arms. She cried against his shoulder, as much in relief as in pain, and if his embrace was more brotherly than it had been before, she couldn't blame him.

She told Dave about Rex Collier, her private investigator, then retrieved the letter and watched him read it. He took his time, and when he set it between them, he said, "Sounds like my grandfather, doesn't it?"

"Ultramoral, ultrastrict—yes, unfortunately it does."

"But this R doesn't mention a brother. It almost sounds as though R were an only child. On the other hand, he doesn't mention a mother, either, and Grandmother Bloom died before her sons did, so that rings true."

"How about the handwriting?" she asked.

"Do I recognize it? I don't believe I've ever even seen a sample of my uncle's handwriting. Maybe the captain would know."

"Maybe. But I don't know how to ask him."

Dave nodded. "I don't blame you for being nervous. No matter if you are or aren't his granddaughter, the captain will come unglued when you tell him your suspicions."

"And that's all they are," she said.

"The Serenity part is the clincher, though, isn't it?" he asked as he picked up the letter again. "If he named the boat after your mother or allowed Ron to do so, then he must have known the two of them were close, maybe even that Serena was pregnant.''

"And yet after Ron died, he didn't do anything for my mother. I don't think he ever tried to find me."

"He hardly acknowledged me till I came hunting for him," Dave said. "He's not overly long on sentiment."

"But he loves you now," Anne said.

"And if you're Ron's child, he'll love you too," Dave added. He paused, thinking. "You're going to have to ask him."

"I know." She pushed her hand against her forehead and added, "Maybe I should just leave the ship, right here, right now." She felt more tears stockpiling behind her eyes and willed them to stay where they were. Her head throbbed with the effort.

"I don't want you to leave," Dave said softly. He looked up, his eyes vulnerable, and ran his hand through his hair. "I really don't want you to leave."

"I don't want to leave," she assured him.

"This idea of a family is really important to you, isn't it?" he asked.

Not nearly as much as it had been before she fell in love with Dave, Anne realized. But she was too close to the truth now to turn away, and they both knew it. There was no way for them to build a future without the truth. She nodded. "This is my last chance."

"If I'd been a little older, I might have heard something," he said, as much to himself as to Anne.

"You never heard rumors about an illegitimate baby?" she asked.

"At four years of age? Not hardly. Maybe Mom did, but I believe she's in Florida—"

"We'll ask her if and when it comes to that," she said,

interrupting. "I don't suppose you recognize my mother's name, either. She and Ron Bloom definitely went to school together."

"I'm sorry," he said. "I don't remember her name ever being mentioned, but I was so small. What about her friends? Wouldn't they know what boy she was friendly with? I mean, it sounds as though she were a sensitive girl—she must have had several friends."

"She started that school in the middle of her junior year. Her parents had just moved to Washington from Kansas. Rex Collier talked to one or two women who vaguely remembered my mother as a quiet girl with few friends. No one even remembers if she dated. She was there for five months; then she was gone."

He shook his head. "Poor kid."

"I know. But she met Ben Moore less than a year later, and they were the happiest married couple in the world, so it did work out in the end."

"Then she was lucky," Dave said. He picked the letter up again, and Anne took another sip of brandy. She welcomed the raw burn as the liquor traveled down her throat. It gave her something to concentrate on besides her confusion and unhappiness.

Dave looked back at Anne's face, and she saw him searching for clues to her identity, just as she did every time she looked at Samuel Bloom or, for that matter, at Dave himself.

"Maybe we're cousins," he said.

"Maybe," she agreed.

He splashed another measure of brandy into his glass and swore softly, more with disappointment than anger. She knew just how he felt.

"You have to talk to my—or is it our—grandfather. You have to find out."

"Yes," she said, dreading it more now than ever. No matter; when the opportunity arose, she'd ask.

Dave shook his head and swore again.

Chapter Ten

T he tall main mast stretched to the top
of the sky. A huge white canvas tri-
angle arched out over the blue Pacific and hummed with
the tension of the wind. Five sea gulls beat their way toward
shore, their wings distant dark victory signs against popcorn
clouds. Strong white sunlight drenched the world, creating
glares and shadows that taxed the eyes.

Toward the east, the California coastline formed a hazy
brown line. Toward the west, a small lump the captain
promised was Santa Catalina Island was still pincushion-
size. The air bordered on hot, but the brisk wind cooled it
down. Anne shaded her eyes and stared mindlessly at the
deep water as though answers lurked in the depths.

"I don't pay you to lollygag around the deck in your
shorts, young lady," Samuel Bloom said, his voice tight.

Anne stood quickly, stumbling as her ankle buckled beneath her. The captain snatched her arm with a viselike grip
and saved her from plummeting over the side of the boat.
She felt the pinch of his fingers linger above her elbow long
after he dropped his hand.

"I was between meals and dishes," she explained. She'd
also been between Dramamine tablets, but she didn't tell
him that. "I guess all the good weather and the exciting

118

sail got to me.'' Mentally she kicked herself. Determined to make the man like her, she'd managed to irritate him instead.

''I am sure that if you were to look around the galley, you would find additional chores and—''

''Look! A shark!''

Anne and Captain Bloom looked simultaneously toward the bow, where Irene was on her knees, pointing toward a spot ten feet off the port side.

A shiny dark triangular fin moved silently through the water, followed by a smaller triangle eighteen inches later. Then Anne saw the black shape beneath the fins.

''It's probably just a little blue shark,'' the captain said.

Irene looked back at him and asked, ''Will it hurt us?''

''Hardly,'' he said but softened the bite of his tone by laughing. ''Maybe if you were right in the water with him and he were a little bigger, he might take a nibble.''

Anne smiled at Irene, but she was as amused by the question as the captain was. The little guy would need a boarding ladder and an Uzi to hurt a human on a boat as big as the *Serenity*.

''That makes eight whales, three sea otters, umpteen jellyfish, fifty some odd sea lions, and a shark,'' Lily pronounced. She and John were sitting next to Irene.

''My wife is keeping count for you, Captain,'' John said as he directed a tender look toward Lily. ''But, honey, you forgot the pelicans.''

The shark disappeared. Anne saw her opportunity to do likewise and hobbled off down below decks.

It was their fifth day aboard *Serenity*, and even though every day had been as unlike the one before as was possible, everyone seemed to have formed certain patterns. Irene and Liz hung around Dave and Skip. The Fontaines hung around each other. Patty Hygrade spent seatime strapped in her bed or bundled in the cockpit, her skin slightly green. She never ate while the boat was moving. Boris hung around Irene or the captain, or Anne if she wasn't fleet of foot enough. The crew entertained the guests, kept the boat moving, cooked, and cleaned.

Dave and Anne exchanged numerous loaded looks but very few words. They stepped aside instead of brushing against each other when passing in the narrow confines of the interior, and Anne noticed Dave no longer found excuses to touch her arm or hand or sling his arm around her shoulders. She knew it wasn't anger that modified his behavior, but fear of his own feelings, and she understood this. Still, with Quince gone and Skip increasingly busy entertaining Liz, she couldn't help feeling lonely.

Catalina Island was twenty-two miles off the California coast, one of eight Channel Islands. Anne had never seen it, and as she cooked dinner, she made frequent quick trips above deck to see if they were getting closer. Dave noticed.

"We won't be close enough for you to see anything till after dark," he said. He was on watch. The wind snapped his dark hair away from his face. Anne's heart gave a now familiar lurch.

"Great."

"You're really anxious to see it, huh?"

She shrugged. "I've always liked islands."

"This one is not a tropical paradise," he pointed out. "It's dry, for one thing."

"Still, it's an island. What's the plan?"

"We'll pick up a mooring in Avalon Bay, then tomorrow morning ferry everyone ashore. The passengers are spending the night at one of the big hotels overlooking the bay, at a place called the Avalon Bluewater Inn, so tomorrow night you won't have to fix a big lunch or dinner."

"What about the crew?" she asked, sensing her opportunity for a heart-to-heart talk with Samuel Bloom was on its way.

"The Hygrades asked the captain to be their guest, and he accepted." He read the disappointment on her face and added, "Maybe you can . . . talk . . . to him in San Diego."

"I guess so," she told him. His skin had bronzed in the heavy sunlight, setting off the healthy whites of his eyes. Anne looked away from him and added, "So, what are you and Skip and I going to do tomorrow night?"

"I'm staying ashore too," he said.

She looked back at him. He was busy studying the compass. "You are?"

"Yes." Irene chose that moment to come into the cockpit. Dave looked at the pretty blonde, and then Anne saw a tinge of red steal up his neck and suffuse his tanned skin, and she realized Irene had something to do with Dave's decision to stay ashore.

Anne felt her heart drop to her toes. She made herself smile and looked away from the dark secrets in Dave's eyes, secrets that told how he felt about this. Secrets she didn't want to know.

"Skip will be here with you," Dave said as Irene went down below into the cabin.

"Good," Anne said breezily as she looked around the deck, anywhere but at Dave.

Daylight was fading fast. John and Lily were on the foredeck having cocktails with the captain, whose back was to Anne. A lasagna—thank heavens for directions printed on the back of pasta cartons!—was bubbling away in the oven. The salad was easy to throw together. Skip and Liz were entertaining Boris in the salon, and Patty was tucked into bed, waiting for the boat to drop its anchor, when she would once again spring back to life. Everything was normal except the lava coursing through Anne's veins.

Had Dave so quickly decided to return Irene's attentions? Could she blame him? She stole a casual peek at him and found his gaze had wandered out to sea, out beyond the dark shape of the island, out where the sun was plunging toward the horizon in a riot of orange-and-purple streaks. She decided that the galley floor could use a good scrubbing and went below to drown her pain in soap and water.

"To John Quincy Adams!" Patty Hygrade toasted as she raised her wine glass.

"Hear, hear," the captain said as he clicked his glass against hers. "Remember, though, before you waste your sympathy and good wine on the old goat, he's getting an all-expenses-paid-for vacation in a lush hospital under the tender care of one Miss Maria Ynez, registered nurse."

"So it's Maria now," Dave noted.

"Well, I spent a long day there, don't forget," the captain reminded him.

"And is his leg going to be as good as new?" Irene asked.

"He may end up with a colorful limp," the captain said.

Anne smiled as she uncorked another bottle of Pinot Noir and set it on the table in front of the captain. They'd picked up a mooring an hour before, and everyone was enjoying his meal as *Serenity* gently swung on her mooring and lived up to her name. Anne made her way back to the galley and the ever-present stack of dishes.

The large inflatable rubber raft dipped and rolled as Anne stepped in. It was crowded with people and overnight bags. The *Serenity* suddenly looked huge when the perspective was almost water level. She watched the black sailboat get smaller as Dave buzzed the Zodiac to the dock. This was his second and final trip. The first load, which included most of the passengers and the captain, was waiting by the boardwalk for Dave, Anne, Skip, and Liz to join them.

Anne hadn't expected a busy tourist mecca, though the proliferation of boats in the harbor should have warned her. She had her own key since only she and Skip were going back that evening. Once ashore, she and Skip made plans to meet back at the dock at four that afternoon. She had to reassure him three times that no, she would not get lost, and no, she would not forget. Liz finally tired of his mother-henning and dragged him off toward the boardwalk. Anne watched Dave, the captain, and Irene follow them. She swallowed hard and started hiking toward the beach.

She found a private spot on the beach after a mile or so and sat down on the coarse sand. Waves pounded onto the golden beach, sighing and hissing as they spent themselves and regrouped for another effort of the eternal onslaught of water against rock.

During her walk Anne had collected a pocketful of small shells. She admired the cowries and limpets, trying to keep her mind full so it wouldn't drift to thoughts of Dave, that rotten, two-timing— Okay, she was pouting. Part of her wanted to get on one of the frequent powerboats that raced between L.A. and Catalina and go back to the mainland, then make her way north to Seattle, to home. She wouldn't go so far as to say she missed the Christmas boutique, but she did feel miserable, and it was all because of Dave.

He sure hadn't wasted any time crying over her, had he? She'd been hurting for days as she tried to come to grips with falling in love with a long-lost relative. It had taken him twelve hours. Anne threw the shells against a big black rock, struggled to her feet, ignored her ankle, and continued walking.

By the time she made her way back to the Zodiac, Anne was limping again, covered with sweat, saltwater, and sand,

and completely exhausted. She was looking forward to a hot shower and a light supper. She waited till five o'clock, and Skip still failed to show up. It was almost dark by this time, and she had decided that Skip had found it difficult to leave Liz's side and had forgotten all about her. Her stomach reminded her it had been a while since breakfast.

"You need something, ma'am?"

She turned to find a short man in a huge cowboy hat. The rest of his clothes leaned toward nautical. He was standing on the dock next to Anne with a portable gas tank in his left hand and a child by his right side.

"Not really," she said.

"Sorry to bother you," he said. "Robin and I saw you standing there when we went to buy this here gasoline, and seeing as you're still here, we figured maybe you were lost."

"Not lost," she said with a smile directed toward the child, who had aroused her curiosity. For the life of her she couldn't figure out if the kid was a boy or a girl. Short brown hair, snub nose, white T-shirt, red shorts, about six years old. There was nothing to indicate gender, not even the name.

The man tipped his hat. "If you're okay, then, me and Robin will get back out to our boat. Almost suppertime."

"You're anchored out there?" Anne asked, pointing toward the bay.

"Forty-foot Hatteras," he said proudly. "Twin diesels. Got over here in ninety-nine minutes."

"That's wonderful," Anne said uncertainly. She looked into the crowds, still didn't see Skip, and made up her mind. "Would you be able to give me a ride back to the boat I'm on?"

He grinned from ear to ear. "Why, sure! Glad to help. Come on, Robin. Let's take the lady for a little ride."

Robin grinned, exposing a blank spot where a tooth used

to be. Anne borrowed a piece of paper and a pencil and wrote Skip a note, which she tucked under one of the Zodiac's oars, carried in case the engine conked out. *Gone back to Serenity—Anne,* it said. She followed the cowboy and his child to their dinghy, and within minutes was back aboard *Serenity.*

"Thanks," she called.

"No problem, ma'am," the cowboy hollered as he gunned his engine and took off toward the opposite side of the bay. Anne returned the child's wave.

It was really strange being aboard *Serenity* by herself. She lit the lamp, took her shower, ate a bowl of vegetable soup, read part of a book, wondered what to buy in San Diego for the rest of the trip's meals (deciding a good cookbook was the first investment to make), and tried not to worry about Skip. By midnight she admitted defeat: She was worried.

It wasn't like him not to come back. It only took a few minutes to zip out and back. After bugging her about being careful, it was hard to believe he'd gone off and forgotten.

But what should she do? She knew where everyone was staying, but the last thing in the world she wanted to do was get Skip in trouble with the captain. If she could work the marine radio in the captain's room, she could maybe call the inn and ask for Liz. Surely Liz would know where he was. But she'd never operated a marine radio, and she had no intention of invading the captain's stateroom again.

She pulled on a pair of jeans and decided to just get ashore and worry about it once she was there. On deck she discovered the problem with this plan: The Zodiac was still on Catalina.

Patience eventually paid off. Within a half hour, a small boat with a quiet engine passed *Serenity's* bow, and Anne hailed it.

"Ahoy! Could I pay you to give me a ride to shore?" she called.

The boat slowed down and came alongside. A woman's voice answered. "Did I hear you right? You need a ride to shore?"

"Yes," Anne told her. She couldn't really see the woman, just a pale face looking up at her in the moonlight.

"Happy to give you a lift, but I'm not coming back tonight."

"That's okay," Anne said as she carefully made her way down the boarding ladder and into the small wooden skiff. "I won't need a ride back."

The woman started the engine again and pointed her boat toward shore. Anne wished she'd put a coat on over her sweatshirt and thought of all the things she was going to say to Skip when she found him.

It was almost three o'clock by the time Anne reached the Avalon Bluewater Inn. It sat on a hill of sorts, overlooking the bay. Anne was huffing and puffing, to say nothing of limping, as she finally reached its front door and walked into the tiny lobby.

A woman with stark-white hair sat behind the oak desk. Her fingers moved deftly as they worked on a piece of needlework. "No vacancy," she said.

Anne walked over to her. She was surprised to see the cross-stitch consisted of tall pine trees and a raging river. "I'm aboard *Serenity*," she said.

The woman looked up for the first time. She peered at Anne over the tops of her half glasses and repeated, "No vacancy."

"But I don't want a room. I'm trying to find someone, and I was hoping a woman staying here as a guest would be able to help me. Her name is Liz Franklin."

The woman shrugged. ''Name doesn't sound familiar.''

''Could you check?''

With a noticeable sigh, the innkeeper put her needlework aside and opened a book. She scanned the page and said, ''Did you say something about the *Serenity*?''

''Yes, that's the boat's name.''

''Rooms 18-21 are booked under that name,'' the woman said as she slapped the book closed. ''A man named Samuel Bloom is the only individual mentioned. Can't help you.''

Anne stared as the woman reclaimed her cross-stitching. Well, it made sense. Samuel Bloom would book the rooms weeks in advance, and unless she wanted to knock on each door, she was just going to have to accept the fact that Liz had chased the promise to meet Anne from Skip's head. Besides, he was a big boy, and what he did ashore was none of her business.

''Thanks for your help,'' she told the woman, who nodded curtly and once again didn't look up.

Anne trekked down the hill, finally figured out how to start the engine on the Zodiac, and went back to *Serenity* to spend the rest of the night alone.

Chapter Eleven

Anne sat in the cockpit with a cup of coffee. The sun had risen two hours before, peeking above the island like a shy child, then blazing forth and bathing the world in rich yellow light. She was unsure what to do about everyone on shore. Had the captain and Skip made previous plans for going ashore and giving everyone a ride back to the boat? It seemed likely. When, though? It seemed so unlike Skip to neglect his duties. Anne just hoped the captain wouldn't blow up at her when his plans were off kilter. Eventually she put on a pair of shorts and an oversized shirt and took the Zodiac back to shore.

One by one the crew and passengers straggled back to the dock area. Patty and Boris were holding hands and wearing new T-shirts—neon orange with the word *Catalina* sprawled across the chest.

"Are we all here?" the captain asked at last.

"Everyone but Liz," Dave said. He was wearing a light-gray sweater the same hue as his eyes. Anne had never seen anyone look so good in gray. He caught her staring at him, and she looked away. Irene, who was slightly off to the side talking to Lily Fontaine, perked up.

"I saw Liz eating a hot dog with Skip," she volunteered. "I guess it was about two yesterday afternoon."

"You mean you haven't seen her since yesterday afternoon?" the captain asked. "Wasn't she supposed to room with you?"

"She never came in," Irene said. "I had the room all to myself."

Anne looked at Dave. He winked at her, and she felt her cheeks redden. He'd known all along that she thought he was staying with Irene. Nice of him to reassure her!

The captain looked horrified. "Are you saying Liz is missing?"

Dave said, "Skip might know where she went." He looked around, apparently noticed for the first time that Skip hadn't come ashore with Anne, and added, "Where is he?"

Captain Bloom turned his glare to Anne. "Please don't tell me he brought Liz back to the *Serenity* and spent the night with her there," he softly pleaded.

"He didn't," Anne said with certainty. Unable to sleep, she'd spent half the night changing the sheets in the guest rooms—one of Skip's jobs and one for which he now owed her—and the other half in the cockpit.

Lily cleared her throat. "I know where they both are," she said quietly.

"Well?" her husband prompted.

"I guess it's okay to tell now. I promised I wouldn't until this morning—"

"Lily!"

She smiled nervously. "Oh, all right. They've eloped!" Her eyes were shining with undiluted delight.

No one said a thing. Anne sneaked a peek at the captain and for the first time understood a phrase Ben Moore used to say often: "He was spittin'-nail mad!"

"Are you sure?" Dave asked.

"Oh, yes. I saw the two of them getting on that hydrofoil for the ride back to the mainland. When I asked Liz what they were up to, she confessed they were running away to get married. She said they'd decided on the spur of the moment. Isn't it romantic?"

Anne saw the corner of Dave's mouth twitch. The captain looked apoplectic. Boris and Patty agreed that it was romantic, and Irene bit her bottom lip and looked thoughtful.

"Well," Dave said with a sigh, "I suppose the rest of us might as well get back on the *Serenity* if we're going to get to San Diego by nightfall."

With a general murmur of agreement, everyone headed toward the Zodiac. Only the captain stood rooted to the ground, his mouth half open, unbelieving. Anne touched his sleeve and said, "Come on, Captain. We'll sort it out later."

He blinked, opened his mouth, closed it, took one last look up the hill as though Liz and Skip might suddenly appear, then grudgingly came along.

The three remaining crew members got the anchor up, and the *Serenity* headed southeast toward San Diego. Anne was delighted with her field promotion to deckhand, though she fully understood that once the sails were up, it was down into the galley for her, lunch to make, dishes to scrub.

Samuel Bloom cornered her and Dave down below decks. Irene and Boris were at the wheel, he explained briefly, his eyes making frequent darting looks toward the hatch. "To make a long story short," he said, "we're up a creek without a paddle."

"Why?" Anne asked innocently.

"We're shorthanded," Dave pointed out. "We could

stand losing Quince or Skip, but losing them both was a blow.''

"Call Dillion when we get into town," the captain told Dave. "Let's just hope he's available for a week."

"Dillion?" Anne asked.

"Old friend of ours," Dave said. "Met him in the Caribbean last year. He helped us bring the *Serenity* through the Panama Canal. He's kind of a flake, though. Are you sure you want me to call him, sir?"

The captain sighed heavily. "Do we have a choice?"

"Maybe Skip and Liz will be waiting for us once we're ashore," Anne said.

Captain Bloom jerked to attention. "Explain yourself," he barked.

"Well, they went off on a lark, didn't they? An unplanned, spontaneous lark. For all we know, they came to their senses before they even reached the mainland. And even if they did get married, all their stuff is still aboard *Serenity*, so they'll be back."

"That young man will never walk these decks again!" the captain bellowed.

Dave looked down at the cabin sole.

"But you need him," Anne said softly.

"I do not need a deckhand who runs out on my boat in the middle of a job," he said. "That kind of conduct is inexcusable."

"Captain—" Dave began, but was cut off short.

"I'd do the same to you," the captain said. His voice was low, but furious and determined, and Anne knew he was speaking the truth. "You are my flesh and blood, but if you abandoned this ship and endangered these customers and this boat, I'd do the same to you." His face was flushed with anger. His hands were tight-fisted balls at his sides. He nodded curtly, message delivered, then with tight, stiff steps made his way up the ladder. Anne and Dave exchanged long looks. Anne was thinking that if she was going to throw another giant monkey wrench into the works, she'd better be prepared to leave the *Serenity* in San Diego, and she knew with heart-wrenching certainty that she wasn't ready for that. She had no idea what Dave was thinking.

"Maybe the captain is right," he said at last.

"About Skip? He's just a kid. This is probably the first time he's fallen in love and—"

"I wasn't thinking of Skip," Dave said. "I was thinking of you."

Stymied, Anne just looked at him. She was so caught up in defending Skip that she missed the glittering twinkle lurking in the depths of Dave's eyes. At last she said, "What do you mean?"

He shrugged. "Just that maybe a girl crew member is a jinx," he said, then ducked when Anne threw a dish towel at his head.

Anne had never been in San Diego before. It was hard to believe that at home, in the Pacific Northwest—in Seattle, Washington—it was most likely raining, maybe even snowing. Hard to believe it was February here and not May or June. The sky was blue, the clouds were cotton puffs, palm trees rustled in the breeze, the air smelled of hibiscus, gulls squawked. Nice.

The *Serenity* motored past the police dock at the tip of Shelter Island. "Why are all those boats tied up there?" Irene asked. "Are they all under arrest? Is it drug smuggling?"

Anne saw Dave look away quickly, but she caught the way his mouth tended to twitch when he suppressed a smile.

"Not at all," the captain said politely. "San Diego is a port of entry into the United States. You have to check in and go through customs. And some of those boats are just taking advantage of the inexpensive rates the city charges for a limited number of days.''

''Then we'll be docking there after we get back from Mexico?'' Patty asked.

''No. We'll run straight from San Ignacio Lagoon back to Monterey,'' Dave said. ''Monterey is a port of entry too.''

''And where are we going now?''

''The San Diego Mariner's Club. We have reciprocal privileges there. Believe me, folks, you are going to love it. We're only here this afternoon and tonight, then tomorrow morning we leave for Ensenada, Mexico, to officially enter Mexican waters.''

They weren't tied up at the yacht club dock more than an hour before the commodore of the Mariner's Club welcomed the *Serenity's* crew and passengers to San Diego. He was a tall man in his sixties, with pale eyes in a ruddy face. His hair was gray and cut into a short crewcut, giving him a military look, enhanced, no doubt, by his clipped voice and formal manner.

''I want to invite you all to the winter dinner/dance,'' he said, including the captain and Anne in his offer. Dave wasn't on board. He'd left after securing *Serenity's* lines, and Anne had heard him tell the captain something about ''digging up Dillion.''

Irene laughed. ''Sounds like such fun! I haven't dressed up in a week now.''

Anne looked at Irene—gorgeous as usual, this time in an ivory silk pantsuit—and sighed.

Lily grabbed John's hand. ''Can we go, honey?''

''Of course,'' he said with a fond smile.

134   *Sail Away!*

Boris stuck his hands into his shorts pockets and said, "Not much for dances, Commodore. Thanks all the same."

Patty hitched her hands on her waist and narrowed her eyes. "Boris Hygrade, if you think for one moment I'm going to miss a party on dry land when a week of sea duty is staring me in the eye, you're absolutely, certifiably crazy!"

He laughed. "Don't get your dander up, old girl. If you want to go, we'll go."

All eyes seemed to swivel around to the crew. "I wouldn't dream of refusing your hospitality, Commodore," the captain said. "The crew will have to make it an early night, however. Early sailing time tomorrow, you know."

"Fine, fine," the commodore said. "Just come in the front entrance and tell whoever is at the desk that you're all my guests. They'll be expecting you. Ladies. . . ." With this, he nodded and left.

As everyone dispersed, the captain took Anne aside. "Billy had connections with a store near the club," he said. "He'd call in his needs, and they'd deliver what he wanted right to the boat. The store is named Delmonico's, but I don't know exactly how he did it."

"I would rather go to the store myself," Anne said. She wouldn't have had the slightest idea what to tell someone on the phone.

"Good. Dave is taking care of ordering from the liquor store we always deal with, so don't worry about wine or replenishing the brandy supply. You take a taxi." He pressed twenty dollars into her hands and added, "This is for transportation. We have an account at the store." He dug into his pocket and produced a laminated card. "Use this thing. It's like a charge card there."

"What about the laundry?" she asked. Immediately she

wished she hadn't because the laundry brought Skip to mind, and the captain's face clouded over like a stormy morning.

"Dave took the ship's laundry with him," he said tightly. "I've already advised our passengers that they can have their personal laundry picked up and delivered back here within hours."

"That must cost an arm and a leg," Anne observed.

"That's not your concern," the captain said stiffly, once again drawing a line in the sand and daring Anne to step over it.

She backed up. "I'd better get going."

"Yes," he said.

"Stop at this bookstore, but don't go away," Anne told the cab driver. "I'll be right back." She was as good as her word, flinging herself back into the cab a minute or two later with a book entitled, *Gourmet Cooking Made Easy*.

As the driver took her to the market, she thumbed through the pages, scribbling hasty notes, trying to formulate a menu for anywhere from eight to ten people for seven more days.

Three hours later she and another cab driver carried twenty bags of groceries down the dock. She tipped him heavily and began the arduous chore of shelving this, re-frigerating that, finding room in the freezer for twelve cornish game hens, six pounds of veal scaloppine, six pounds of pink salad shrimp, and a whole salmon. There were vegetables to clean and sort, cheeses to rewrap, spices Anne had discovered while speed-reading the new cookbook on the way to the store.

The grocery bill had been staggering, and already Anne could think of a few things she had forgotten and would have to pick up in Ensenada. Meanwhile, theoretically, she had enough food aboard for one hundred servings of break-fast, lunch, and dinner.

Her ankle, which had conversely stopped bothering her after her hike around Catalina, had decided to remind her it was there and was throbbing with a slow, steady beat. She used a bare arm to wipe the sweat off her forehead and leaned back against the stove.

"There you are."

Anne looked up. Dave was grinning at her from the main salon. He held a box full of assorted liquors. She opened the door into the engine room and stood aside as he stored the box inside the small compartment. When he came back into the galley, his eyebrows rose at the mess.

"Cinderella isn't going to get to go to the ball if she doesn't hustle," he said.

"Cinderella is pooped," Anne replied. She wondered how he managed to look so good in a pair of cutoff blue jeans and a red T-shirt.

"Anything I can do to help?" he asked.

"I wish I knew enough to know what I'm missing. Everything seems to be in order, which kind of scares me because I'm sure it's not."

"You need confidence." He leaned forward and touched her hair. When his hand came away, he was holding a brilliant purple flower. Anne remembered the bougainvillea bush she'd brushed against on her way down the dock with the groceries.

"The captain told me we'd all been invited to the big dinner/dance up at the club. Are you looking forward to it?" he asked.

She took the papery petal from his fingers and pretended touching him meant nothing. "I can't go to that party," she said. "I didn't bring the right kind of clothes, and besides, I've got a lot more to do in here before I'm ready to dance the night away. Did you find out about your friend?"

"Dillion? Yep. He's between jobs, as usual. He'll be here tomorrow morning, bright and early. And you don't need fancy clothes," he added. "These affairs are always a mix of jeans and tuxedos. Besides, I don't go in for all that razzle-dazzle. I'll dress in my shorts if you do."

Anne looked down at her feet. Dave tilted her chin up till their eyes met. "What's wrong, honey?"

"Don't call me that, Dave. It's hard enough."

"Cousins can be quite affectionate," he said softly.

Oh, if only it were that easy! She decided a change of subject was definitely in order and said, "I was thinking about Skip. I thought he and Liz would show up here today to get their belongings."

Dave dropped his hand. "Well, Skip has to know how the captain feels. He's probably planning to contact me when we get back to Monterey. Don't forget he knows our schedule. By the way, the captain called the hospital. Quince is doing fine."

"I've been meaning to ask. Well, that's a relief."

"Come to the dance," Dave said suddenly.

Anne shook her head. "No."

He lowered his voice. "I want to hold you in my arms. I want to smell your hair and kiss your neck. I want to have one evening when I can legally and morally cuddle you, Anne, before you can talk to Granddad, before you confirm that we are long-lost cousins and we have to look at each other and not touch. Is that too much to ask?"

She smiled at his wording and nodded. "Yes." Not because she didn't want those same things, but because she did want them—wanted them way too much. "You go ahead," she added. "I have all . . . all this galley stuff to . . . to organize."

He stared at her. "Maybe you're right," he said at last. He ran his finger down her cheek, turned, and left.

The galley was a popular spot. A half hour after Dave left, Anne looked up to see the captain staring at her. She'd heard his voice out in the salon, talking to the passengers. She'd even prepared a tray of preparty, predinner hors d'ouevres, made easy as she'd bought every item premade.

"Anne," he said after clearing his voice.

"Yes, sir?"

"I guess I forgot to tell you I called Santa Barbara and checked up on that old phony, Quince. He told me to tell you he's sneaked his pipe twice, both times under the nose of Nurse Ynez."

Anne smiled, a sudden stab of loss reminding her how she missed Quince's humor. "Dave told me he was doing okay," she said.

"Yes. He says he's running three-legged races up the hall with that poor nurse." The captain smiled—not a common occurrence!—and shook his head. "She should get a medal for putting up with him."

"How long does he have to stay in the hospital?"

"I don't know. Several weeks, anyway. Good thing Dillion is available. Well, I just wanted to pass along Quince's message. I know how much he likes you and how close you got to feeling toward the old rascal."

Anne waited while the captain studied the ceiling and cleared his throat again. He obviously had something else to say, and she was curious. As she waited, she studied his face. She'd never noticed the myriad of fine lines that fanned out from the corners of his eyes and mouth. He always seemed so robust, she forgot to think of him as aging. She suddenly felt an overwhelming urge to tell him who she was. She wanted to feel his sturdy arms around her, know he'd accept her. She took a deep breath and waited.

"You've turned out better than I had any right to expect," he said at length. "Quince said you would, said he saw something of me in you, whatever the blazes that means. You're good to have aboard, girl, and I guess I just thought it was high time I told you so.''

Anne bit at her lip. Tears stung her eyes. She tried to hold them in, but they spilled down her cheeks.

''Now, now,'' he said awkwardly. He put his hand on her shoulder, and she took a clumsy step forward. The tears continued. The captain drew her a little closer, and then he was hugging her, patting her back, his body stiff and un-yielding and yet warm and strong too.

Anne cried harder then ever. Her lips formed the word ''Grandfather,'' and she said it silently, like a prayer, and it filled her heart.

Chapter Twelve

D ance music floated over the marina.
The Mariner's Club was built of dark
wood and smoky glass, and lights twinkled around the well-
lit building like thousands of fireflies. Anne sat in the cockpit
alone. She imagined Irene—who had produced a knee-
length satin gown and a diamond necklace from somewhere—in Dave's arms, and though she fought to keep her
thoughts and hopes focused on the captain, she felt a deep
stab of jealousy.

"Anne? Is that you?"

Anne recognized the voice immediately. "Skip?"

"Over here," he said. He was little more then a dark
shadow on the dock. "Are you alone?"

"Yes? Are you?"

She saw the shadow come closer and climb into the boat.
His face was lit by the full moon, and she saw the familiar
grin curve his lips.

"Liz is at the hotel," he said as he sat down beside Anne.

"Are you—did you—"

"Get married? Yep."

"Oh, Skip."

"I know it was sudden," he blurted out. "The thing is,
Anne, I really love Liz. But her father is a real snob. She

140

didn't think he'd allow her to marry me if he knew I wasn't anything more than a deckhand on a sailboat, so we decided the only thing to do was to elope. We rented a car last night and drove to Vegas. We just got back here an hour ago.'' He paused. His eyes looked huge in his face. Anne saw him run his hand through his tight curly hair. She knew he was working on adding something, and she had a fair idea what it was, so she waited.

At last he coughed into his hand. ''Is the captain . . . mad at me?'' he asked.

Anne nodded. ''Furious.''

Skip swore under his breath. ''I knew he would be.''

''I wish you hadn't burned your bridges quite so thoroughly,'' she said.

''I guess it was dumb. Well, what is, is. I just came back because I need my stuff.''

''I'll help you,'' she said.

''Better not,'' Skip cautioned. ''If the captain knows you helped me, he'll be twice as mad at you. Why don't you take a walk?''

''No. You've been my friend, and I'm not going to sneak away and leave you to pack up alone. Let's go.''

It was the first time Anne had been in the forepeak, and she felt like a naughty child sneaking in where she didn't belong. The area was taken up with one large head and four bunks. While the workmanship wasn't quite as nice as it was in the rest of the boat, the crew quarters were, nevertheless, attractive and relatively spacious.

Dave's bunk was apparently the one farthest aft. Anne recognized his gray sweater folded on top of the green spread. Above his bed were pictures, some of a fair-haired woman of about fifty with a cat cradled in her arms, and two of Dave and the captain standing next to each other, the *Serenity* visible in the background.

"This is my bunk," Skip said. His looked like all the others. He opened a drawer built into the bottom of the bunk and took out a canvas bag, which he began stuffing with the clothes he yanked from his allotted three drawers.

"What can I do to help?" Anne asked.

"Uh—how about taking those things off the wall? Put them in here." Skip pointed at a pocket on the side of the bag. He went into the head to retrieve his belongings.

Anne took down a calendar of old wooden sailing ships. She noticed with amusement that Liz's name was written in on the very day she set foot aboard the *Serenity*. He'd used red ink and underlined it twice. There were also a few pictures and a small bark painting done in primary colors. Anne stowed them and turned to see Skip coming out of the head. His eyes looked sad.

"Hard to believe this isn't home anymore," he said. "I've been aboard almost two years now. I've been up the inland passage, down in the Bahamas, even took her to Hawaii. I'm really going to miss the old girl."

"And the captain," Anne added softly.

"Yeah. And Quince and Dave, and even you, Anne, though I know you're only aboard for another week."

"Yes," she said. Was that all? One more week and she would be driving back to Seattle and that rotten little store?

"Good-bye, Anne," Skip said suddenly.

"What are you and Liz going to do?"

He was anxious to get off the boat—Anne didn't blame him—and he climbed the ladder back on deck. He gave her a hand up, then walked quickly down the deck toward the ladder to the dock. She hurried to keep up with his long strides. When he spoke, his voice was low again and drifted back over his shoulder.

"Liz and I are going to open a little sailing school in Los Angeles. At least, that's what we want to do. I've saved a little, and money is Liz's middle name. She loves to sail, you know.''

''I know.''

''Yeah. Well, this is it. We'll get Liz's things in Monterey. Say good-bye for me, will you? Maybe by the time next week rolls around, I'll have enough guts to talk to the captain and try to explain. I don't regret marrying Liz, but I guess I didn't go about it very well. Take care, Anne.'' He kissed her cheek, then clattered down the ladder and quickly blended into the shadows, disappearing up the dock.

''Good-bye,'' Anne called out after him.

They reminded Anne of a neighborhood coffee klatch. Each had one fin stuck skyward from the sea. Beneath the fins, the long, dark shapes of their bodies floated on the surface. They were sea lions or seals—she was always getting the two mixed up—and they were soaking up the first warm morning rays. She had no idea why they floated with one long fin pointed up, or why they gathered in a group of nine or ten.

The *Serenity* had left San Diego at five A.M. It was dead calm then, and it was dead calm now. Anne had fixed a quick crew breakfast of scrambled eggs and toast, but none of the guests were up yet. She suspected they were all sleeping off last night's party. The captain was behind the wheel, and Dave was up on the foredeck with Dillion. They were setting sails and taking them down again in rapid succession, as the canvas tended to hang in limp, dejected folds. Anne wondered why they couldn't accept the simple fact that there just wasn't any wind.

Dillion wasn't quite what Anne had expected. Tall and slender, his shoulder-length blond hair caught in a rubber band at the base of his neck, he moved in his own long-legged grace. His eyes were light-blue, which probably accounted for the fact that he wore sunglasses, which dangled from a red cord around his neck when he wasn't wearing them. A small gold earring glittered in his left earlobe. He was dressed in khaki shorts and a white T-shirt, and though he'd only had time to direct one quick "hello" toward Anne, he'd managed to suffuse it with a surprising degree of sensuality.

He and Dave made quite an eyeful. Dave was a little shorter, a little heavier and more muscular, a lot darker. They were opposites in looks, and yet the same quick humor seemed ingrained in both. Anne supposed Dillion was the more attractive, but he didn't send her heart spinning into cartwheels the way Dave did.

Even though the dusty coastline was more than three miles off the port side, Anne could see occasional flashes of bright metal in motion. She put on a pair of sunglasses and peered at the coast.

"There's a highway leading from the States to Ensenada," Dillion said. He'd come up behind her and put his hand on her right shoulder. It appeared he wasn't cursed with shyness.

"They're getting there a lot faster than we are," Anne observed.

"Hmm—but not with the same panache," he said slowly, his easy smile in place.

"Don't need to convince her of that," Dave said. "Anne has a real feeling for the sea. Don't you, Anne?"

Anne looked at Dave, who was staring at Dillion's hand resting casually on her shoulder, and inwardly she smiled. "Yes," she said simply. She turned her attention to the captain and added, "Sir? May I please take the helm for a little while?"

"There are galley duties and—"

"Mexican omelettes for breakfast," Anne interrupted.

"The eggs are ready, vegetables chopped, cheese grated, muffins ready to heat. All that's missing are the diners, who are still asleep. Please, just for a few minutes."

He grumbled. Anne smiled and moved toward the helm. Dillion said, "You might as well let her. Just like every woman ever born, this one will eventually get what she wants."

Anne decided to ignore this chauvinistic comment as the captain appeared to respond to it. He gave Anne the wheel, showed her the compass heading, then watched her with his eagle eye while she managed to stay right on the mark. Since the wind was still dead and the ocean had the surface texture of a mill pond on a quiet day, this feat didn't require a lot of talent.

The captain nodded and made a big show of being annoyed that she was helping with the watch, then sauntered off along the broad wooden decks toward the bow, his easy gait a dead giveaway he wasn't as perturbed as he acted. Unaccountably Anne's heart filled with fondness for him as she began to detect a heart of oatmeal beneath the crusty exterior.

"If he's not careful, you're going to wind him around your little finger," Dillion told her.

"And if I'm not careful, he's going to decide he likes her better than me and throw me off at the next port and hire her on as first mate," Dave added.

"He'd never do that," Anne protested.

"He can't," Dillion agreed. He put his free hand on Dave's shoulder and added, "You're related to him, buddy-boy. Blood is thicker than water and all that."

Dave and Anne exchanged long glances.

"On the other hand, she's a heck of a lot prettier than you," Dillion added.

Dave cast him a pseudo-withering look and stalked off after his grandfather.

Ensenada Bay was crowded with Mexican fishing boats, sail boats and motorboats from the United States and Canada and beyond, and old derelicts. The *Serenity* dropped her anchor a little out of the way of the main traffic. Anne noticed several large moorings and wondered aloud why they just didn't pick up one of them.

"Take a look at the seaweed hanging off the chain," Dave told her. "They don't pull the moorings and check them every year or two. You don't want eighty Thousand pounds of boat depending on an old engine block and a rusty chain."

"This is my first foreign country," Irene said softly. Her eyes were glowing with excitement.

"But not your last," Dillion prophesied. He was busy lowering and securing the mizzen sail, which had done little more than flap uselessly all day. Perversely the wind had started to come up the second the anchor hit the water.

"Have you ever been to Mexico?" Dave asked as he threw Dillion a cord to secure the sail. It took Anne a second to realize he was talking to her. "No," she said. "I've been to Canada a couple of times but never south."

"Some people don't like it here," Dillion said. He leaned against the mast and folded his arms across his chest. "They say it's dirty and smelly and dusty. But I like it. It's not sanitized like the States. You get the feeling that people really live here and not all behind closed doors and fences."

"Life spills out onto the streets here," Dave agreed. "But there are so many tourists, you have to wonder if the government isn't going to try to clean things up. I hope not."

Irene laughed. "I guess I'd better go ashore and see this place before it turns into Los Angeles," she said.

"I'd be honored to escort you," Dillion said and melted away any opposition she might have to that idea with a five-hundred-watt smile.

They took a "taxi" to shore. The captain paid the friendly skipper of the small motorboat that transported them to a wooden dock with American dollars, which the man seemed more than happy to accept.

Upon landing, Irene and Dillion immediately took off for a tour of the sights. Patty and Boris invited John and Lily to have dinner with them, and the two couples walked off after Dave made arrangements with the boat taxi to ferry everyone back to the *Serenity* as they came back to the harbor. The captain issued prolific warnings to one and all not to get lost.

Anne joined Dave and Samuel Bloom for the walk to the port captain's office where they would officially enter Mexico. As they walked along the colorful wharf, Anne felt a sense of contentment stealing over her. She loved these two men, and she didn't want to lose them. She looked over at Dave, and he smiled at her, as though he were reading her mind.

A small burro munched dry grass in a nearby field. The captain stopped to look at it, his habitually stern expression softening.

"What are you thinking about?" Dave asked.

"Nothing," the captain grumbled.

"Come on, Captain. There's actually a hint of a smile on that mouth of yours. Anne and I deserve to know what's responsible for it."

The captain shrugged. "Memories. You get old, and memories are apt to leap up and bite you at any given second."

"And what is this memory?" Dave prompted. He followed the captain's gaze to the burro. "That donkey?"

The captain resumed walking. "It's a family thing. I don't want to bore Anne with it."

"You won't," she assured him quickly. She saw Dave smile at her, and she looked down at the path.

Several more quiet seconds passed as they walked; then the captain sighed. "I brought the boys down here about 1960. Frankie was twelve or thirteen; little Ronnie was eight or nine. It was hot, real hot. I had a little yawl then, named the *Susan Star* after the boys' mother. That was a nice little boat, Dave. Planked with Doug fir and— Well, never mind. We had a little cat aboard name of Windy. Every day I'd take the boys into town and we'd buy gooey stuff at the *panaderia,* at the bakery. Your father loved the apple tarts, and Ronnie liked these big, sloppy lemon-filled things. Even little Windy liked the bakery food. Only cat I ever saw that would turn up its nose at fish and tackle a doughnut."

"It sounds like fun," Anne said wistfully. She loved hearing stories about Ron Bloom, but she was afraid to press for details. It was the first time the captain had ever actually spoken to her about things not directly related to the *Serenity* or work, and she was afraid this sudden rush of personal revelations would dry up.

"Fun?" the captain said. "Guess it was. 'Course, those boys got into their share of mischief, I assure you. They 'borrowed' a donkey one afternoon and got lost. I spent most of the afternoon looking for them—finally found them in a lady's garden. Only reason I found them at all was that the boys had fallen asleep and the donkey was eating all her flowers and she was screaming at it."

"Dad and Uncle Ron were buddies then," Dave said.

"Oh, yeah. The years that separated them didn't seem to matter much. Even later, after Frank married and you came along, the two boys were best friends. He was real fond of your mother, Dave, and he was crazy about you."

"Ron sounds . . . nice," Anne said softly. The captain pulled his cap down on his forehead. He looked troubled and Anne added, "Is anything wrong?"

"No," he said quickly; then he sighed and added, "Ron was a good boy."

"You sound as though you're trying to convince yourself of that," Dave observed.

"No," the captain barked. "He was a decent kid—never lived long enough to be a man. But he had some . . . problems . . . before he died, so in the end he wasn't as happy as he'd always been."

"Problems?" Anne questioned softly. She felt a shiver run up her spine.

The captain's eyes assumed a faraway look, as though turned inward toward the past. "Ronnie was only seventeen. Boy that age shouldn't have to worry too much about the future, about family and children." The captain stopped talking. It was all Anne could do to force herself to continue walking.

Dave said gently, "Grandfather, why did Ron have to worry about family and children?"

Only a second passed before Samuel Bloom answered Dave, but in that second Anne's heart stopped beating, her body closed down. She stood rooted to the sidewalk as her mind raced. Here it came—here was the answer. She wasn't ready. She wanted to snatch Dave's question back. She realized with a shattering certainty that she loved Samuel Bloom, that she'd known all along that he was her grandfather, her family. But he would hate her. She'd made his beloved son's last few weeks of life unhappy, and it was something that Anne felt he'd never forgive her for. She took one last look at Dave, casting off the uncousinly tidal wave of love she couldn't help feeling for him, and steeled herself for the captain's answer.

Samuel Bloom cleared his throat. "It's a long story, Dave, and it doesn't matter anymore. If talking about it now could give me Ron back or even let him be the same happy-go-lucky boy he'd been all his life up till that last month or two, well, then I'd yak all afternoon. But we've talked enough about family. Look at Anne. She's so bored she decided to stay behind."

Anne's heart resumed beating in long, painful thumps. She took a shaky breath or two. She tried to smile, but it was too soon. Dave walked back the few steps that separated them and took her arm. "Come on, little cousin," he whispered. "We'll try again later."

The captain had resumed walking. "Here's the port captain's office. You kids coming?"

"Yes," Dave said, tugging Anne along. "We kids are right behind you."

Chapter Thirteen

Four dolphins cavorted beneath *Sereni-ty's* bow. Crew and passengers alike sat or stretched out on the wooden deck, cameras pointed down. Every once in a while one of the dolphins would leap out of the blue water, its body a silvery, sparkling arch, powerful and simple in design, breathtaking in motion.

Only Dillion stayed aft. He'd rigged a fishing pole off the stern pulpit and had already delivered a glistening fish to Anne, which everyone assumed she'd cook for dinner. Anne had spent the better part of an hour finding a recipe and convincing Dillion that he'd have to clean his catch.

Later the captain gathered everyone into the cockpit, where he directed Anne to serve hors d'ouevres. She settled on fresh tortilla chips, spicy bean dip, and cold bottles of Mexican beer. As the passengers ate, the captain told them what to expect in the upcoming three days.

"It'll take us another thirty hours steady sailing to reach the lagoon. The Mexican government has laws protecting gray whales while in Mexican waters. For instance, only two boats at any given time are allowed in the lagoon. We have to be there for our turn or risk losing it."

"How long will we stay there?" Patty asked. She'd re-

sumed her "boat underway" position in the cockpit and
had stopped eating. Anne had foisted a couple of her seasick
pills onto Patty, but the older woman insisted they didn't
help. Anne suppressed a smile every time Dillion had to
manipulate himself around her—her perch was right in the
traffic pattern leading to the stern and his fishing pole.

"We'll be there two days."

"I can hardly wait," Irene said. Since Liz had abandoned
ship with Skip, Irene seemed to be taking over the role of
excited passenger. Or maybe it was Dillion!

"Me too," Lily agreed. "I want to touch one."

Dusk was approaching. The night sky was flooded with
color, and the warm breeze was turning cool. "I'm sure
you'll all enjoy yourselves. We'll take excursions out into
the lagoon— Well, you'll see. Are there any more questions?" the captain asked.

Patty raised her hand. "Do you mean to say that this boat
will be under way for all of tomorrow and tomorrow night?"

"Yes," he said. "But the morning after next will find
us entering San Ignacio Lagoon, and I promise you, Patty,
the whales will make up for everything."

"Maybe you'd be more comfortable down in your bunk,"
Dillion suggested as he stepped over Patty's abandoned
sunglasses and paperback book, took his fishing pole from
the rod holder, and began reeling in the line.

"I assure you, young man," Patty said with a flash of
her eyes, "that sitting outside all day is preferable to rolling
around in my bunk like a beached whale with a stomach-
ache."

Anne could see Dillion reassessing Patty Hygrade as he
slipped the pole back into the holder. Until that moment
he'd written her off as a neurotic old lady, but with her
colorful description, she came alive in his eyes, and he bent

his long legs and sat on his heels, his face only inches from hers.

"How about I make you up one of my famous deep-sea cocktails?"

"It won't help," she said, then added, "What's in it?"

He slapped his hand against his chest. "My dear woman! I wouldn't divulge the secrets of this elixir were I dragged behind a Navy torpedo boat."

Patty giggled. "What the heck," she said at last.

"Just don't poison her," the captain told Dillion as the latter slid by him on the ladder. The captain looked around, spied Anne and Irene leaning against the cabin top and added, "Anne, you go and keep an eye on him."

Dillion grabbed Anne's hand. "What a splendid idea! Come along, lovely lady. You can be my lab assistant."

"Lucky girl," Dave said dryly, his gaze directed toward Dillion's hand clamped around Anne's. He held a bucket, into which he was putting empty beer bottles.

Dillion laughed. "Anything for science—right, Anne?"

"Right," she said as she was half lifted down the companionway ladder. "What's in this elixir of yours?" she asked.

"Booze," Dillion said. He patted the top of the liquor cabinet and found the key.

"How did you know the key was up there?"

"Didn't you?"

"No."

He shrugged. "Last time I was aboard *Serenity,* Billy was the cook. Trust me—he knew where the key was!" He opened the cabinet, loaded four bottles into his arms, and carried them into the galley.

"I need O.J.," he said as he unscrewed the lids.

Anne took a pitcher of orange juice from the fridge. She

glanced at the ship's clock and saw that it was time she started baking Dillion's fish. Thank goodness she'd bought a dozen lemons in Ensenada. The only recipe she would even attempt aboard the boat called for three lemons, two cloves of garlic, a cube of butter, and handfuls of herbs.

He poured half a glass of orange juice, a dollop of brandy, half a jigger of vodka, a whole jigger of dark rum, and a splash of gin.

"Are you sure that won't hurt her?" Anne asked.

He shrugged again. "Probably put her sound asleep. Let's dump an egg in it, too, so she gets some protein."

"Can't. Have to cook eggs, Dillion, or run the risk of infecting someone with salmonella."

"Women," he said with a hint of disgust. "You take all the fun out of things."

"Do we?" she asked as she helped screw the lids back on the liquor bottles.

"Well, not entirely. For instance. . . ."

Anne looked up in time to see him looming above her. Startled, she took a step back. He reached out and gripped her shoulders, and then he leaned down and kissed her.

She supposed it was a good kiss. He certainly seemed to know what to do with his lips and his hands, but as far as arousing her feelings, she might as well have been kissing the fish he reeled in hours before. Dillion must have noticed her lack of response, because he let go of her and narrowed his eyes.

"You don't like being grabbed and kissed," he stated.

Anne thought she heard a door closing somewhere up forward. She brought her attention back to the attractive man in front of her and said, "I'm not entirely opposed to it."

"Then you don't like being grabbed and kissed by me."

"No," she said. "Sorry."

"You have devastated my ego," he said with a twinkle in his eye.

"I doubt any woman could accomplish that feat this easily," she answered.

"Hm—" He stirred the orange liquid and tasted a spoonful. "Whoa! That ought to do something to the old gal. Want a taste?"

"I think I'll pass. I have dinner to cook and a whole life ahead of me."

"Think maybe my masculine charms will work better after dinner or maybe tomorrow?" he asked.

"No," she said with a smile.

He picked up the glass and walked away from the mess he'd made, but before he disappeared from the galley, he turned back to Anne and said, "Dave was right about you."

"Oh?"

"Yes," he said, and then he was gone.

The next thirty-six hours passed slowly and uneventfully. The sail was timed to reach San Ignacio Lagoon in the early morning. Anne spent night watches with Dave, semi-content to be in his company. Patty went below decks with the dark and, thanks mainly to Dillion's potent knockout drink, seemed to be able to spend a moderately comfortable night in her bunk. It was one of the few times Anne and Dave could be alone, and Anne craved it even though both of them kept their hands to themselves and the conversation impersonal.

Still, the night air was almost warm and the stars plentiful, and, as Dave had admitted days before, he was a romantic. Several hours before daybreak on the morning they would finally reach San Ignacio Lagoon, he put the boat on autopilot and sat down on the seat beside Anne. His leg touched hers, and she moved away a little.

"It's not as though we'll both spontaneously combust if we touch each other," he said softly.

She smiled. "I know. But if we fall in love, Dave, it's only going to hurt worse when we can't have each other."

"It's too late for that. You know it, and I know it. We're already in love. And it only gets better or worse, depending on your point of view."

"I didn't mean for this to happen," she said. "All I wanted was a father, a family. I know this is hard for you to understand, but this is my last chance. There are no leads past Ron Bloom. I won't go as far as saying that I still hope the captain is my grandfather, but if he is, then we'll just have to make the best of it." Such noble words, she thought to herself. Words were easy, action much harder.

"At least you'll never be alone again." His voice was firm. "You'll always have me."

"As a cousin? It's going to drive us both nuts."

"Can't we get married, anyway?" he asked.

She felt as though her chest was constricting. She took a deep swallow. "Dave—"

And then his lips were touching hers, setting them on fire, melting her heart. She kissed him back with a longing that terrified her. If she could have merged into him and disappeared, he still wouldn't be close enough. She was crying, and he kissed away her tears and stroked her face, and she felt tears on his cheeks as well. She struggled with herself, finally turning her face away. "You told me you wanted two kids and a house on the ocean," she mumbled.

"I want you more," he whispered into her ear.

"Now. But in the years to come? Listen, Dave, it's against the law for first cousins to marry, and genetically we shouldn't have children together. We'd have to keep our relationship a secret, even from the captain."

"I don't care," he said, his kisses trailing down her neck.

"Not now. But sooner or later we'd both care. I have to know the truth. I have to know if we're cousins."

"Of course we are," Dave said. "The captain as much as told us that the other day."

"I have to hear it from his lips."

"But, Anne—"

"One of us has got to use our heads," she said firmly.

"And not their hormones, is that it?"

She took a deep breath. "More or less."

His lips were against the hollow of her throat. "I don't think I can stand the thought of being your cousin. I know I couldn't stand by while another man falls in love with you. When I see Dillion looking at you, it makes me want to—"

"The kiss was just empty flirtation," Anne said, remembering the sound of the closing door.

He straightened up. "He kissed you!"

"Didn't you know?"

"No. Put him on the same ocean with a pretty girl, and he switches into pursuit mode. He's impossible."

"I think he's fun," Anne said.

"Great. I suppose he's a terrific kisser."

"He's not bad."

Dave sighed.

"He's not you, though," she added.

He put his hand against her cheek. "He just better stay away from you, that's all."

"So you can admit you witnessed the big kiss."

"But I didn't. I would have smashed in his nose if I had."

Then who closed the door? Anne shrugged that issue aside and asked, "What exactly did you tell Dillion about me?"

"Oh, well, I told him you were stubborn. I told him you were as hard as nails. I'd tell him you slept in combat boots and grew a beard every night if I thought it would help."

"Help what?"

"Keep him away from you. He tends to like his women soft and compliant."

Anne took Dave's hand in hers and held it against her cheek, wishing on the fading stars for something she couldn't begin to name.

Chapter Fourteen

I t was ten o'clock in the morning when *Serenity* motored into San Ignacio Lagoon and dropped her anchor in three fathoms of sparkling blue water. The wind blew gently from the east, warmed by the desert. To the northwest, isolated sand dunes towered over the desert, and the line between lagoon and sky shimmered and blurred in the distance. Across the lagoon another boat swung on her anchor.

Anne had spent the night before making sandwiches and refrigerating them so that lunch would be ready on demand. She did not want to take a chance of missing the first excursion out onto the bay to see the whales. Even from the deck, she could see one several hundred feet away, its huge, mottled body rising perpendicularly out of the water and slamming back down with a gigantic splash.

Dave and Dillion inflated the rubber raft and threw it overboard while the captain outfitted everyone in life preservers. Anne felt as though she were sandwiched in an orange.

Dave jumped into the raft, and Dillion handed him the small gasoline outboard engine, which Dave secured to the stern. Then one by one the two young men helped the passengers board. The captain came last, right after Boris

159

and Patty. Patty, who had come back to life as soon as the anchor hit the water and was now munching a handful of cookies, closed her eyes as the captain lifted her down to Dave and Boris and didn't open them until she was sitting on the floor of the boat.

John Fontaine had given Lily the camera, and she was eagerly snapping photos of everyone and everything. Dillion sat in the bow with Irene, who seemed to be making a big deal out of not looking at him or laughing at his stupid jokes. Anne sat in the stern with Dave and John Fontaine, and in the middle the captain was surrounded by Lily, Patty, and Boris.

Dave motored away from the *Serenity*. The little raft jounced and jiggled as they slowly motored across the rippled surface of the lagoon. The engine sounded like a wounded mosquito as it pushed the boat along, and Anne liked the way the speed whipped her hair away from her face and the salty breeze stung her cheeks.

"Over there," Dave said suddenly, pointing toward a large, dark shape in the water. The whale seemed to change direction and come toward the raft. Dave slipped the engine into neutral, and the small boat bounced along the surface before finally slowing down and drifting with the current. "I think they're attracted to the noise of the engine," he said as the whale continued swimming closer.

"I'm surprised at this current," John said. "Isn't it kind of hard on the calves?"

"Gets them in shape for the long migration north," the captain explained. "They'll leave here in April sometime."

The whale was much longer than the dinghy. Three feet from the boat it poked its head up out of the water, exhaling noisily through two blowholes. A powerful burst of water sprayed the raft and its occupants as the women all squealed in delight. Anne thought for a moment that their noise had startled the huge animal, for it sank beneath the surface again. Seconds later it resurfaced, this time even closer. He (she?) rubbed its head against the raft. Lily was the first to reach out and touch it. Anne wished she had a camera, sure that the expression of pure joy on Lily's face was something John would want to capture and remember.

Anne touched the whale. Its skin felt like a rubber beach ball. Colonies of crustaceans and whale lice mottled its gray hide. Knuckles ran down its back. Dave was busy pointing out even more details, but she was too caught up in the excitement of meeting her first whale to listen closely to his words. All she could see was the big eye that stared at the funny occupants of the boat, and she wondered which species, human or whale, was studying which.

"The first friendly whales were noticed in this lagoon in 1975," Dave was saying. "Great little ambassadors for their own survival, aren't they?"

"Hardly little," Boris said. He was rubbing the whale's head. Anne thought that if the whale were a cat, it would be purring.

Suddenly the whale slipped under the water again. A chorus of disappointed sounds rose from the raft; then Lily almost screamed.

"Over there. Look! Oh, John, they're coming this way!"

A big whale and a small whale were swimming toward the raft. The mother slowed down and seemed to push the baby toward the humans, just like a patient mother nudging her darling toward strangers, gushing, "He's a little shy, but isn't he adorable?"

The calf popped out of the water and pushed against the raft, which bobbed gently away. Patty was on her knees and fell back into the raft, landing soundly on Boris. They both broke into laughter and scrambled back into place to admire the newcomers.

"I feel like we're little more than a giant bathtub toy for the little guy," Dillion said.

"Isn't it a dear little thing?" Patty said, totally captivated by the friendly face.

All hands reached out. This whale was smooth and dimpled, its skin darker than the adult's. As it raised partially from the water and eyed its admirers, the mother rolled in the warm water, sunbathing, it seemed, her eye half closed against the glare of the sun.

"They like us touching them," Anne said as she patted the slippery calf.

"Yes, they do," Dave agreed. "They spend hours touching each other during their mating rituals. They'll spend hours rubbing against our boat and and letting us rub their skin. They just like to touch." His eyes met Anne's eyes, and he smiled.

"He's adorable," Irene said suddenly. Up till that moment she'd been still, but now she stood, one knee balancing on the rubber pontoon, and reached out to run her hand down the baby's back, her sapphire rings echoing the blue depths of the water.

"Please, Irene," the captain said. "Sit down."

"He's so adorable," Irene said, ignoring the captain, but more because she was so wrapped up in the whale than because she was being contrary. She reached out farther, her calf muscles flexed. The mother chose that moment to dive under the boat. The raft scooted backward in her wake. Irene would have fallen backward into the boat if she hadn't tried so hard not to touch Dillion. As it was, she ended up in the water beside the boat, surfacing immediately, thanks to her life vest, spitting water out of her mouth, her hair plastered over her eyes.

The calf was startled by this sudden change in the game rules and disappeared after its mother.

"You okay?" the captain asked as he leaned down and took one of Irene's hands.

"She's fine," Dillion said as he gripped the other hand. He laughed and added, "That was quite a nosedive. I bet you were on your school diving team, right?"

Irene glared at him. Most men would have melted under the intensity of her glare, but not Dillion. He threw back his head and laughed again. Then he unceremoniously dragged her back aboard.

Irene pulled a long strand of bright-green eel grass out of her hair and spit saltwater over the side of the boat.

"Are you all right?" the captain repeated.

"Fine," she said, casting a murderous look at Dillion.

"We'll go back for lunch and to let Irene change clothes," the captain said. "Then this afternoon we'll take you all over near the shoreline where you can see the mangroves."

He helped Irene sit down. Dave started the engine. Lily leaned over the bow and pointed at a small pod of whales a great distance from the boat, and three pelicans swooped overhead. Anne studied the way Irene ignored Dillion and the way Dillion didn't seem to notice.

The dinghy left again two hours later, sans Irene and Anne. The former said she wanted to spend the afternoon in the cockpit where she couldn't possibly fall overboard. Anne had a fancy dinner to create and was busy down in the galley, laboriously following the recipe for brandy/apricot glaze, which she was supposed to "drizzle" over the Cornish game hens at just the right second.

She carried a steaming mug of hot tea on deck a little while later. Irene had looked as though she could use it.

"Why, thanks," Irene said as she accepted the tea. "I

know the water isn't very cold, but it really shocked me, falling in like that.''

Anne sat down on a seat across from her. ''I can imagine.''

Irene's long hair was almost dry. She pushed it behind her ears and took a sip of hot tea. Anne was suddenly conscious of her hiking shorts and red T-shirt covered with a rather messy galley apron. It was hard not to notice clothes when the woman sitting across from you was recovering from her ocean dip in a caftan that looked as though it were sliced from a rainbow.

''Dillion shouldn't have laughed at you,'' Anne said.

Irene raised her eyebrows and nodded. ''No, he shouldn't have. I felt humiliated enough as it was.''

Anne shrugged. ''He's just like that.''

Irene set the mug on the deck and said, ''You seem to know a lot about Dillion. I was under the impression you just met him.''

''I did. But I've met men like Dillion before. Haven't you?''

''No.''

Anne looked down at her hands clasping her knee.

''I mean,'' Irene elaborated, ''that no man has ever laughed at me before. My mother would have had him shot!''

''She sounds like a real tiger,'' Anne said, a little startled.

''She runs an airline, so I guess she has to be a tiger.''

''But didn't you run into men like Dillion in school or—''

''I went to private girls' schools on the East Coast,'' Irene said. ''Daddy died when I was little, and Mother never remarried. I guess I'm not used to men.''

Anne thought of the way Irene had been leaning on Dave and found this shy-little-girl act hard to swallow.

"He doesn't care about money or position. He does what he wants to do when he wants to do it. It's disgraceful." Irene looked disgusted.

"As long as he doesn't hurt anyone—"

"What makes you think he hasn't hurt anyone?"

"Has he hurt you?" Anne asked.

Irene nodded slowly. "I saw him kissing you. Just the day before, he'd kissed me and I thought— Well, I guess I assumed—"

Ah, the mystery of the closing door was solved. Anne reached over and patted Irene's hand. "It was just a kiss, Irene. It didn't mean a thing to me, and I think it meant less to him. I think the man is incapable of being around a woman without making a pass."

"I thought he liked me," Irene said, her feelings painfully close to the surface. "I knew all along that Dave was crazy about you, but he was attentive and so handsome, so I just enjoyed his company. But Dillion—he's different."

"Yes," Anne said, but her thoughts had strayed to Dave. Were their feelings that obvious to an outsider, and if they were, did the captain know? And if he did, what in the world would he think when Anne confessed who she was?

"—in love," Irene said. Anne was vaguely aware a sentence had preceded those two big words. She looked at Irene and said, "What?"

"I think I'm in love. With Dillion, I mean."

Anne just stared at Irene. It was on the tip of her tongue to warn her about men like Dillion, but hadn't she just done that? Besides, who was she to ground her heels on budding romance? Just because she couldn't have her man, why should she go around dumping on poor Irene? "Good luck, then," she said at last, and added silently to herself, *You're going to need it.*

Chapter Fifteen

The next day was spent exploring the legal boundaries of the lagoon, watching the whale gazers from the other stateside boat buzz around the lagoon, reaching out to touch the whales that came to greet them, watching the ones that didn't with binoculars. Anne watched in awe as two males and one female spent hours rolling and cavorting near the surface as they engaged in their mating ritual. Misty clouds of spray, rolling dolphins, seabirds, and sea lions decorated the lagoon and kept everyone busy.

The captain ordered *Serenity's* anchor raised early Friday morning. Patty had eaten like a horse the last two days, preparing herself for the long run north the way a camel stores water for a desert crossing. She brought her book and her blanket into the cockpit, took her regular spot, and set up camp. Anne had finally gotten her sea legs and hadn't taken seasick medicine since San Diego.

Two huge whales and four silver dolphins accompanied the *Serenity* out of the lagoon. A large motorboat was waiting outside the entrance. The captain told Patty that it was their turn to enter now, and they all watched the boat replace them with a certain amount of jealousy.

Serenity pounded north, her bow rising to the swells, her

sails stretched to the wind. Dave and Dillion were in their element, changing sails, tightening this line, loosening that one. Anne had spent the last day in the lagoon changing all the sheets, polishing the brass lanterns, scrubbing the floors, preparing two days' worth of meals as far ahead as she could, sewing up a hole in Boris's favorite shirt, and cleaning the galley. She was looking forward to long days and nights at sea. She was not looking forward to Monterey, and she was dreading going back to Seattle alone.

"Penny for your thoughts," Dave said the second evening. Anne was standing on the foredeck, bracing herself by holding onto the halyards. The sea had been building all day, and now saltwater washed down the decks as the boat tackled the waves.

She shrugged. "I was just wishing this didn't ever have to end. I was just wishing the trip could go on forever."

"It can," he said softly. "You've worn the poor captain down, you know. He likes you. Sign on as cook for the trip to Hawaii."

Anne sighed. "I wish I could. But he isn't going to feel the same toward me in a couple of days. And you and I are going to need some time apart."

"I could take a leave—"

"Don't say it," she said quickly, covering his lips with her fingers. That was a mistake. It just reminded her how soft his lips were and how much she enjoyed kissing him.

He stopped talking and hung one arm around her shoulders. Together they watched the sun set on the far horizon.

The trip south had all evolved so slowly, lazily almost, Anne reflected that night as she lay in her bunk. The one thing about being on a sailboat was that one could toss and turn without moving a muscle. On deck, she knew Dave was at the helm and probably wondering where she was. She yearned to go to him.

How in the world was she supposed to go back to that dumb Christmas boutique? How was she supposed to sell snowflakes in July when her heart was aboard this boat? She sat up in bed. She'd talk to the captain as soon as they made port. Dave was right—he was beginning to thaw toward her. He'd probably be delighted to have a granddaughter. He'd want her aboard. She'd stay, and Dave and she would—

The dream fell apart. Dave and she would spend forever looking at each other with longing in their hearts. They would resent any other woman or man who happened along. When one of them fell in love again, the other would die inside.

She lay back down. Then she sat up again. She was still dressed and decided to visit Dave.

The captain was at the table, a hot cup of coffee in front of him. "Can't sleep?" he asked Anne.

"No," she said. "I was going up on deck."

"Just be careful. Barometer is falling—we're in for a storm of some kind. The sea is a little rough tonight."

"Thanks." She climbed the ladder. She grabbed a harness and clipped it on over her sweater.

The night air greeted her with a cool puff.

"Is that you?" Dave asked as she slid the hatch closed. "Yes."

"I thought you weren't coming," he said as she fumbled for the safety line. The boat dipped down the back of a big wave, and she stumbled.

"I'm going to hate night watches for the rest of my life," Dave said, his voice dripping in melancholy. "They'll always make me think of you."

"Thanks a lot." She knew what he meant, though. Where was that safety line?

"It won't be the same—"

His words were lost to Anne as she stumbled again when the next big wave coursed under *Serenity*. Her fingers found the safety line, but before she could pop the clip to secure herself, she was thrown sideways and collapsed on her injured ankle. The boat pitched back the other direction, and she fell toward the sea.

For one long second she knew she was going to end up in the black ocean, alone, a mere speck in the night. Then the lifeline dug into her abdomen and slid down her thighs. She grasped with frantic hands. One found the bulwark. Her head was down toward the ocean; her feet fought the air. Nothing but a tenuous grip on slippery wood stood between her and the sea. She was too scared to scream. The boat rolled back the other direction, plunging her head beneath the water. *Dave!* she cried inside and fought to thrust herself upright and away from the terrifying darkness.

And then big hands grabbed her around the waist, lifted her back into the cockpit, pulled her close.

"Anne—" Dave gasped.

She coughed. He forced her head away from his chest and smoothed back her hair with trembling hands. "Anne," he said again, his voice little more than a hoarse croak. "I thought—"

"I'm okay," she said.

He kissed her forehead and her eyes. He ran his hands down her arms and around the back of her neck, touching her as though reassuring himself she was all in one piece.

"I'm okay," she repeated.

The hatch slid open, and the two of them separated.

"What's going on out here?" the captain yelled.

"Anne almost fell overboard," Dave told him.

"I'm okay," Anne mumbled.

"I'll get her dried off and into bed," Dave said.

"I will," the captain said firmly. "Come on then, girl. It's not as though you actually ended up in the drink now, is it?"

Sensitive to the end, old Captain Bligh, Anne thought, but she supposed he was right. He helped her out of the harness and, with a minimum of fuss and bother, had her tucked into her bunk, her head wrapped in a dry towel. She fell asleep but slept fitfully, dreaming over and over again of falling through the sea, lost in a black abyss.

It was light outside when Anne awoke. She lay still for a few moments, casting the latest dream out of her mind. Dave had grabbed her. She remembered his hands caressing her, remembered his lips, and the fear in his voice. She finally looked at her watch and saw that she'd overslept by two hours.

The boat's movement was jerky and violent. Anne undid the straps that had kept her anchored in her bunk and sat up. Her abdomen hurt where she'd hung against the lifeline the night before, and her ankle was throbbing again. She laughed at her little miseries, just glad she wasn't out paddling in the ocean somewhere, waiting for Dave to find her.

Someone had invaded her galley! Dirty dishes were stacked in the stainless sink. Eggshells littered the garbage, and coffee grounds were finely sprinkled over everything, like powdered sugar over French toast. Most of the mugs were off their hooks, but the ones that remained swung in six-inch arcs as *Serenity* punched her way against the weather. It was still early, but obviously someone had taken it upon themselves to feed an Australian marching band. The remains of this feast sat in the bottom of a cast-iron fry pan, securely locked into place on the stove.

" 'Bout time you woke up," Dillion said. His hands were

full of more dirty dishes that clattered together as he steadied himself against *Serenity's* motion.

"What's everyone doing up so early? What's that smell?"

"I think the storm woke the masses," Dillion said. "And what you smell, pretty lady, is caviar. I put it in with the scrambled eggs. Want some?"

Anne looked back at the frying pan, at the runny eggs littered with black specks. "Pass," she said. "But thanks for cooking breakfast. Did everyone eat?"

"Everyone except Dave. He never has liked my cooking. Even Patty ate it, which goes to show he's just picky."

"You're kidding. With all this motion aboard, Patty actually ate?"

"I have a way with women," Dillion said, his lips curling into a smug smile as he stepped closer.

Anne unloaded the dishes from his arms. "As long as you clean up after her when she loses it," she muttered, sighing at the mess in the galley. Dillion retreated.

By nightfall, the rain, driven by the winds, pounded the decks like nails. Anne thought it a wonder there were no leaks in the skylight. She knew the captain was on watch, and she wondered how he stood the unrelenting force of the element. Everyone else was snug inside *Serenity*. Some were reading; some were watching the storm through the safety of the portholes. Dave was in the navigation room. Anne had made some of Billy's canned salmon into croquettes for dinner, but for once people weren't very hungry and had only pushed the food around on their plates.

She was scrubbing up the last of the dinner dishes when Dave came into the galley. He stood behind her and slid something over her head.

Anne looked at the tiny pendant dangling around her neck. It was a small abalone shell, ringed in sterling silver.

"What's this?" she asked as she turned to face him. She ran a fingertip over the glossy opalescent surface.

"I've had that a long time," Dave said. "I want you to have it."

Anne felt her throat close, and she tried swallowing.

"I'm in love with you, Anne. I've been practicing saying that all night. I love you, I'm in love with you, you're the love of my life. But in the end it doesn't matter how I say it, does it? I'm finding it hell on earth to accept that I can't have you the way I want you, the way you want me, but now, before we reach Monterey and Grandfather welcomes you into the Bloom fold, I want to stand here as a man and tell you that I love you and I always will love you, and there isn't a thing on earth I can do about it."

He kissed her gently, lingering for a moment. She could taste the sadness and resignation on his lips. And then he was gone. She wiped the tears from her face, slipped the shell under her sweater, where it nestled above her heart.

She was shelving the last of the dishes when she heard a noise coming from the engine room and slid open the door. Captain Bloom faced her as he stumbled forward.

His usually ruddy complexion was pale underneath a thin layer of sweat. His voice, between deep breaths, sounded weak.

"I'm sick," he muttered. "Been throwing up the last two hours. Don't know what's wrong. Can't find Dillion. You're going to have to help tonight, and it's messy out there."

She took his arm as he sagged against the counter. "I'll be happy to help, you know that."

"I know." He looked at her in panic and added, "I don't want to upset the passengers, but this feels like food poisoning. What have we been feeding them?"

"Oh no," Anne said. "I gave them salmon just an hour ago. If it's that, it might be botulism."

"Calm down. I didn't eat dinner tonight. Felt too rotten. Besides, it takes longer, and the symptoms are different. What else? Think, girl!"

"Um, shrimp salads and vegetables soup for lunch."

"Same shrimp you used days before? The stuff you have frozen?"

"Yes."

"It's not that then. What else?"

"Dillion made breakfast. Eggs and caviar."

"It was good," the captain said. "I ate a lot of it."

"It could be salmonella poisoning from the eggs," she said, remembering how undercooked the leftovers had appeared.

The Captain nodded. "Well, if it is, at least we're not going to die. But I feel terrible."

And so would everyone else except her and Dave, Anne realized. "Let's go through the engine room and get you into bed," she said.

He straightened up and looked down his nose at her. "Thank you, but I'll take care of that myself. You'd better get ready to help where needed. Dave is in charge now."

"Okay," she said. Once the captain had left, she dug through the garbage. The eggshells were on the bottom. It was a little hard to tell since they'd had other refuse dumped on top of them, but it did seem as though some of the shells were covered with straw and dirt. Anne thought of the runny mess Dillion called scrambled eggs.

She went out into the main salon. Boris was sitting at the table. Tiny beads of perspiration stuck out on his forehead.

"I feel awful," he said.

"I can see that." She felt his brow and confirmed he was running a slight fever.

''Where is everyone?''

''Patty's been in bed since dinner. Irene went to check on her. That Dillion fella looked kind of peaked too. I don't know where the Fontaines are.''

''We're in here,'' John said as he came out of their stateroom. ''Lily feels terrible.''

''How are you?'' Anne asked.

''A little nauseous. I'm more worried about Lily, and I just heard Boris say Patty and Dillion are sick too. What's wrong?''

''It may be salmonella poisoning. I'll look it up in a minute, but if I'm right, you'll feel feverish and nauseated and have diarrhea for a day or so, but it won't last too long.''

''Great,'' John said. ''We go to sea to get poisoned by a chicken.''

''Do you know where Irene is?''

''I think she's tucking Dillion into Liz's bed in her stateroom. He looked worse than Lily.''

''He'll live,'' Irene said from behind John. ''And I'm fine. I already looked up salmonella and traced it to the eggs the big lug cooked this morning. Is that what you think, Anne?''

''Yes. Well, what about you, Irene? Did you eat eggs?''

''Nope. Wouldn't give Dillion the satisfaction of eating his cooking. But I saw the captain eat.''

''He's sick too,'' Anne confessed. ''But neither Dave nor I ate breakfast, and the boat is loaded with electronic gear, so we'll get to port—don't worry.''

Irene nodded. ''You go play Horatio Hornblower, and I'll play Florence Nightingale, only you get the captain. I don't think I could handle him as a patient.''

''Deal,'' Anne said.

Irene lingered as though there were something else she

wanted to say. Finally she touched John on the arm. "Could you possibly help Boris get into his pajamas and into bed?"

"Huh? oh, sure." He took Boris's arm, and Anne thought to herself that John was already looking paler than he had a moment before.

"Anne?" Irene said. "I'm a little worried about Patty Hygrade. I read that medical book on the shelf over there. It says to watch out for dehydration. The rest of us have been healthy, but Patty is so frail, and she hasn't eaten or drunk anything for two days besides the little bit Dillion charmed down her throat. I think she's the one we'll have to watch."

"I'll tell Dave," Anne assured her. "Maybe we can take the boat into a closer port. Do you think anyone here would mind?"

Irene laughed. "Mind? Hardly. It's all part of the adventure, right?"

"Right," Anne said and added, "Irene, I'm awfully glad you're aboard."

Irene looked surprised by her own answer. "So am I!"

As Irene hurried off to check on Dillion, Anne donned foul-weather gear and a harness and went outside.

Mother Nature had unleashed a dandy storm. The sky was black. Rain thundered down in torrents. The sea was huge, sending *Serenity* careening up and down mighty cliffs of water. The wind drove the rain in a slanting diagonal that pooled in the brim of Anne's hat, then poured down her face and her back.

Anne clipped her harness to the safety line, which she found with no trouble.

"You shouldn't be out here!" Dave yelled.

She fought against the wind till she was standing next to him. "The captain told me to help you," she said. "Better not turn me down. I'm the only help you're likely to get. Everyone else is sick.''

He raised his head. The wind blew the brim of his hat straight up, and Anne saw the whites of his eyes widen. ''Really?''

''Eggs,'' Anne said as she gripped the mizzenmast to keep from falling as *Serenity* surfed along.

''Dillion?''

She shrugged.

''I knew he'd get us one way or another. Is that why the captain left his watch early?''

''Yep. Is there a closer port than Monterey? We're worried about Patty Hygrade.''

''We'll make for San Diego,'' Dave yelled. ''I'll set the autopilot. You stay here and keep a watch on things while I go forward and get that headsail down.''

''Be careful,'' she called as he moved away into the dark.

Four A.M. took a few weeks to roll around, or so it seemed to Anne. She sat with the wheel in front of her, the little autopilot clicking away as it kept *Serenity* on a compass course to San Diego. The night was dark and wild and noisy. Dave had spent the better part of it taking down sails and putting them back up to try to ease the motion for the passengers. Now he was down below making coffee. Rain batted Anne's face and conspired with the wind to creep up her arms and legs and down her neck like cold wet snakes.

The companionway hatch slid back, and Dave's form momentarily blocked the light that escaped from the inside. Anne heard the clip of his harness, the slide of the hatch, and the cockpit returned to the dark. He surefootedly made his way aft to her and handed her a mug.

''How is everyone?'' she asked as she cradled the scalding mug in cold hands.

"Not bad. Boris and Patty are asleep, Lily and John are actually reading, and Dillion has his own personal nurse, which is more than he deserves."

"Did you check on Grandfather?" The word *Grandfather* slipped out without a preceding pronoun such as "your" before Anne even realized it. Dave didn't seem to notice.

"He's okay. I promised him some hot soup, but I couldn't find any."

"I'll fix it," Anne said.

Dave caught her arm. "You're enjoying the storm, aren't you?"

She hadn't thought about it till that second, but she had to admit she was. "There's something wild and exciting about it."

"I like 'em too. Better when there's not a boatload of sick passengers."

"They're all being pretty nice about it."

"We'll get them to a doctor and fly them back to Monterey. A few have obligations starting Tuesday. I know for sure that John Fontaine has some kind of big business deal going on in Hawaii next week because he was talking about it the other day."

Anne suddenly realized it was all going to be over in hours rather than days. Dave released her arm and said, "You belong out here, Anne."

"You know I have to go back to Seattle. At least for a while."

"No. You need the captain right now—I don't. When we get back to Monterey, I'm leaving for a year or two. Get a real job, make my mother happy. Maybe by the time I get back, we'll be able to be around each other. Maybe I'll. . . . Well, you know what I mean."

"Yes." But she had no intention of letting him give up everything he loved just for her sake. With a blinding stab of regret, she wished that she'd never come, that she'd let the whole matter rest with her mother and the man who had raised and loved her as his own.

Anne found two cans of soup and dumped them into a saucepan. She added some water and heated it, then took mugs to all the passengers, sensing the captain wouldn't want something until his passengers had it. The Fontaines looked pale and a little ragged but were deep in murder mysteries and accepted the broth gratefully. Boris helped Anne coax some of the warm fluid into Patty. When Anne told them how sorry she was they were ill, they brushed aside her apologies.

"These things happen," Boris said.

Patty touched Anne's hand and added, "I didn't want to tell that sweet young man, but I threw up most of his breakfast. You won't tell him, will you, dear?"

"I promise," Anne said, flooded with relief.

Irene was sitting on Liz's bed, Dillion's head in her lap. She was stroking his long, fair hair, and Anne felt such jealousy—not about Dillion, but the freedom these two had to love each other—that she almost dropped their soup.

"Thanks," Irene said.

Dillion noticed the tears in Anne's eyes and said, "You had your chance, honey. Looks like Irene has me now."

"Just drink your soup and shut up," Irene told him.

Anne knocked on the captain's door. No answer, so she gently pushed it inward. The captain was lying on his bunk, an orange blanket thrown over his body. Anne could see he was still dressed and knew that it would take more than a little food poisoning before he'd relinquish the reins on the *Serenity*.

He turned his head and opened those piercing eyes. "Come in. Is that the soup Dave promised?"

"Yes. Would you like me to help you take off your shoes? Dave and I are doing fine outside."

"I bet you are. No. I'll leave my shoes on. Just hand me the soup."

Anne gave him the mug and watched as he sipped the warm broth. He looked up and motioned at the built-in seat by the small desk. "Sit for a moment," he commanded.

Anne looked over her shoulder. "I really should go help Dave. He's so tired—"

"He's used to being tired on a night run. Don't fuss over him. Besides, the sea is calming down. Can't you feel it?"

"Now that you mention it—"

"Going to have to develop a sea sense if you're to stay aboard *Serenity*," he said.

That did it. Anne sat down. "But—"

"You're turning into a pretty good cook," he added. "No Billy—not yet, anyway. On the other hand, you don't drink everything in sight, either. Am I right in thinking there's something going on between you and my grandson?"

"No! Well—"

"You have to speak your mind," he said.

"I'm trying," Anne snapped.

The room fell as quiet as any small room on a boat in the middle of a storm at sea ever does. "I can't stay aboard," she said. "I . . . I have a small boutique in Washington, and I have to get back to it."

"Hogwash," the captain said. He swallowed the last of his broth and pushed the empty mug toward her.

"No, it's true," she protested, taking the mug and clutching it to her chest. "It may sound silly to you, but I . . . I like the boutique and—"

"You belong out here," he interrupted, "not in some

stuffy store. The sea is in your blood. I've been roaming her for years, and I can tell when someone is meant to be on dry land and when someone is meant to be on a boat. You are meant to be on a boat. You've got just enough good sense to know that. Remember, you were the one who came to the *Serenity* asking for a job you weren't any more qualified for than I was. But you made it work, all right—I have to hand it to you. I respect that kind of determination in a person.''

Anne felt tears sting her eyes as she looked at the captain's haggard face. She could feel the tiny abalone shell on her skin, rising and falling with each breath. She looked around the cabin, knowing he spoke the truth, knowing that she truly had come home, and also that she was going to have to leave. She wouldn't wait till Monterey. She'd leave as soon as *Serenity* got to San Diego, and she'd never, ever look back.

Her gaze drifted to the picture of the captain's family, especially to the face of his youngest son. Ron Bloom. The captain was right—there was no way to get him back, and he alone was responsible for Anne being there. And he was gone long, long ago.

''Those are the sons I was talking about,'' the captain said. ''The oldest one is Frank, Dave's father. The younger is Ron. I think Dave kind of looks like Ron.''

She stood and peered closely at the photo. ''Yes,'' she said finally. ''He does.'' She was at the door when she realized she couldn't walk out of that room in the same state of confusion she'd walked in. She took a deep breath, turned around and said, ''I didn't come here, I mean to the dock in Monterey, to sign on as your cook, Captain Bloom.''

He didn't flinch. ''Explain yourself,'' he ordered.

''I came because I wanted to find my father, and I thought you might know him.''

"What's his name?" He propped himself up an elbow and waited expectantly.

Anne came back toward the bunk. She felt strange, almost calm. It was as though she were at the end of the line and there was nowhere else to go and nothing else to lose. She said, "Ron Bloom."

Silence. The captain sat up. He narrowed his eyes. "Is this some kind of sick joke?"

"No." She stood awkwardly, her heart pounding. "My mother went to the same school as Ron. They were classmates. She was a year younger than Ron. She got pregnant, and someone with the initial R promised he'd marry her, told her he loved her. He never did, and as you well know, your son died a few weeks later. You said he was worried about having a family. A few months after he died, I was born."

"When?" he barked.

"The following January."

He counted the months backward on his fingers. "So your mother was pregnant in May."

"I guess."

"And you think Ron was your father and that I am your grandfather."

"Yes."

"And do you want it to be so?"

This wasn't what Anne had expected. "Yes," she said truthfully, "and no."

"Hm—" He held his stomach and groaned but brushed aside her concern. Anne thought to herself that she sure knew when to hit people with shocking news. *Wait till they're sick and then spring yourself as a long-lost relative. Great tactic.* She mentally kicked herself.

"My parents died a couple of years ago," she said, trying to explain, trying to fill up the silence. "They were the only family I had. I started looking for my biological father when I found a note he'd written. It doesn't matter what the note said. What mattered to me was that I might have another family somewhere else. I guess I never really thought about all the lives I'd be disrupting.''

''And all you have to go on is this R business?''

She didn't want to tell him how his son had described him. What was the point? It would only hurt him. ''That and the name of your boat,'' she said, ''and the fact that you said Ron was worried about children and family before he died. It all fits.''

To her great surprise, Samuel Bloom took her hand and pulled her toward the bunk. She perched on the edge next to him. When he spoke, his voice was more compassionate than she would ever have thought possible.

''Ron was a good boy. He had lots of friends, got pretty good grades, was real fond of his brother's family. I couldn't blame him. His own mother had died when he was little, and Frank's wife, Dave's mother, was nice to Ron. I didn't much care for the woman, but after Frank died, she did a good job raising Dave all by herself, so I guess I was wrong.

''Anyway, the spring before Ron died, he got a dandy case of the mumps. He was just recovering from another illness, and his resistance was real low. Doctor said that's why the mumps hit him so hard. He had these high fevers and swollen glands—Well, it doesn't matter now. By May he was over the worst, but the fool doctor told him that because of the fevers, he'd probably never have babies of his own, and that knocked the kid on his ear.

''Why that doctor had to tell him that— Couldn't he have just let nature take its course? Ron had wanted his own family since Frank got married. He kind of idealized the whole thing, know what I mean? He was crazy about little Dave, and then he had this steady girlfriend named Kathy or Katie—something beginning with a K. They had all sorts of plans. Stupid doctor took the heart out of him.''

Anne was having a hard time assimilating what the captain was telling her. It was as though the information were hung up in a logjam inside her brain. She asked, ''That's why he was worried about his future?''

''Of course. Listen, Anne, what with that infection and then the mumps, Ronald missed lots of school. He had his heart set on marrying that girl of his, and then he gets sick, and in June he finds out he can't have kids. He was sullen. He would have gotten over it in time, but the waterskiing accident kind of cut his time short and he didn't have a chance.''

Too many emotions were churning in Anne's stomach. She looked again at the family portrait, at Ron's face, an echo of Dave. Of course she'd sensed familiarity in the picture—Ron looked like Dave. It was Dave she saw, not some shadow of herself.

''One thing,'' the captain said. ''It was little Dave who gave Ron the mumps. He had a real mild case, but they hit Ron hard. I never told Dave because I didn't want to. . . . Well, you know.''

''I think I do,'' Anne said softly, loving the captain more and more by the second.

''What's this about *Serenity*'s name?'' he asked.

It took Anne a few moments to answer. ''My mother's name was Serena, and my father called her Serenity. And then, when I saw the name of this boat, I put two and two together—''

''And got six! I bought her with this name. Liked it, so I kept it.''

''You're not my grandfather?'' Anne said, needing to state it plainly.

He patted her hand. "I'm not your grandfather. Couldn't possibly be your grandfather."

"And Dave is not my cousin."

"No."

She could hardly believe it. She'd been so certain. Maybe if she'd waited till she could afford to send Rex Collier, she could have spared herself and everyone else. But if she'd sent him, she'd never have met Dave. . . .

Anne threw her arms around the captain's neck. Relief flooded her eyes, and she sobbed against his chest for a moment. She could feel him tense, knew how uneasy she was making him feel. She pulled herself together and pushed away from him. "I'll try not to cry on you again," she mumbled.

He nodded as though he thought that a very sensible idea. She got to her feet and walked to the door.

"Anne?"

"Yes?" she asked, turning.

"In a way I will be your grandfather, won't I? When you and Dave get married?"

She felt as though the sun were burning its way through her chest, escaping in brilliant beams through her eyes and her lips when she smiled. "Yes," she said.

"So I guess you can cry on me. Not often, though."

"Thanks."

"Just tell Dave not to get so wrapped up in you that he forgets to keep the boat on course. I'm going to stay down here for a while longer yet."

Anne watched him lie down. She knew she would abandon her search for her biological father, that she'd been parented by the best of men and now had a future with two more men she loved with all her heart. A person shouldn't be so greedy.

*   *   *

Dave had turned off the autopilot and was behind the wheel. The captain's instincts had been good: It did appear as though the storm were abating. The rain wasn't trying as hard, and the silvery waves looked a tad smaller. Anne clipped her harness onto the safety line and made her way to Dave.

"Why did you turn on the outside lights?" he asked.

She shrugged. She'd wanted to see his expression when she told him the good news. She was trying to think of some clever way to say it.

"Sun will be up in a while," Dave said. "Look off to the horizon—see that patch of gray? A couple of little stars have been peeking through there, winking at me, promising me today is going to be beautiful." He paused and looked upward.

Anne knew that their impending separation was eating away at his gut and his heart and that she really should get off the stick and tell him the good news.

"I figure we're three or four hours from San Diego," he said.

The boat coursed down the face of a swell. Anne's insides rose into her throat the way it did when an elevator dropped too fast. She smiled. "Dave?"

"How's Patty Hygrade?"

"Not too bad. She told me she threw up most of breakfast, so I don't think we have to worry too much about her. Dave—"

"Good. And Grandfather?"

"Your grandfather is fine." She paused and added, "By the way, I talked to him?"

"Yeah?" His eyes widened, and he added, "You did? You mean about you and him?"

"Yes." She kissed his damp cheek by the corner of his mouth.

Startled, he drew back. "What did he say?"

"About what?"

"Anne, you really can be annoying, you know that?"

"I'll try to be better."

"Good. Now what did he say?"

She ran her finger from the corner of his left eye to the top of his lip. "He said that Ron Bloom could not possibly be my father, that the boat was named *Serenity* when he bought her, and that— Well, I guess that's all."

Dave looked astounded. "He's not your grandfather."

"Well, he did point out that he would be in a way when you and I got married. Not technically, but—"

No more words escaped her lips because Dave had planted his firmly over them and was crushing her in an embrace made all the more difficult thanks to foul-weather gear, harnesses, and hats.

The kiss said everything that was in his heart, and though Anne spent one brief second wondering how far off course they'd end up before it was over, she quickly abandoned all rational thought and turned her attention to the matter at hand. Above, the sun was trying to break through the clouds; the last of the rain splattered halfheartedly on their heads. And in the final equation it really didn't matter to Anne where *Serenity* ended up—she was already home.